AIRWA

Cleve Ochs

Forward

In Airwar Legacy the names are fictional. The characters are real. I personally worked or flew with all of them except for one man who was killed flying in combat. He was a real person and I was able to access his records.

At the time, I was not researching this book, but listened to them tell their stories while we flew and worked on airplanes or fed hay to cattle. I do not know if every detail they told me was true but they were very interesting history. I've had these memories stored in my head for over fifty years so am not responsible for any errors in detail.

Prologue

I was a spectator to the events related in this book. As a three-year-old boy I witnessed the anxiety in the eyes of the adults around me as they crowded around the radio in our kitchen, hearing of the bombing of Pearl Harbor. I had no idea where Pearl Harbor was, but my father's solemn statement that our lives now were going to be very different, sunk into my young mind. I saw many young men leaving, uncles and cousins among them. During the war I saw the stars in the windows of many of the houses in our little town and knew that they represented the price someone had paid for our freedom.

When I visited a cousin in another small town, the local children excitedly explained that one house had five gold stars in the window! Everyone rushed to see it. One boy explained that all five of the young men who had grown up in that house had been killed when their ship had been sunk by the Japanese.

In 1959 I was sent to Germany as a young soldier. Anytime I was free I would jump on local trains and go sightseeing. There followed a series of events over a ten-year period that led me to the writing of this book. All the main characters in the book were men I worked and flew with. None of them are alive now, but they had lived these events and I am only repeating what they related to me in many different settings. Some stories were told in airplanes over Europe, while the other side of the story would be told years later, sitting on a horse or in an old truck feeding hay to cows in Oregon.

That was over a half century ago. Most of these stories were filed away in the farthest recesses of my mind but I knew I could bring them back anytime I needed them. Now they are history. It is difficult to find anyone who will listen to them so it is time to write them down, so they won't be lost.

The first German I met was Kurt. He was responsible for getting me a German pilot's license. He helped me become a member of the Frankfurt Flying Club (*Frankfürter Luftverein*). He was a quiet, soft-spoken man and it was some time before I learned he had been an aggressive fighter pilot who shot down seventy-eight airplanes during the war. He was credited with forty probables and twelve victories flying the jet fighter *Me-262*.

He never bragged about his role in the fighting, but he did excitedly tell me about an American pilot who accidentally came into his store one day. After talking for a while, they realized that Kurt had tried to capture that American, resulting in Kurt being shot down by friendly anti-aircraft fire. He probably held the record for the number of times he had been shot down: seventeen times! He had been wounded twelve times and remarked that he probably had spent more time in the hospital than flying.

Three years later I met Emil. He taught me how to fly correctly. He had seven years of combat experience and would not allow any mistakes in the air or on the ground. It was impossible to surprise him as his head was constantly turning to see if any enemy fighters were sneaking up behind him. He would lecture me about certain maneuvers and always concluded with, "I flew in combat for seven years and was never shot down." I had to take him at his word. German records show that he had eighty-one confirmed victories.

My relationship with Werner was on a more professional level. After all, he had been a general at twenty-nine while I, at twenty-six years old had only been a U.S. Army sergeant. He always referred to me as the "*Ami.*" Once a week we counted the income from the sightseeing flights flown in the previous week. It was a complicated process because my company was a contractor to Werner's company. But my company had more airplanes flying than Werner's, so our part was larger. He enjoyed trying to confuse me and was like a professional gambler with his long fingers and quick moves. Regardless of these small irritations I was always aware that he was an extremely brave man who had tried to protect his comrades in arms from an insane leader.

Hans was the only character in the book who I never met, since he had been killed in combat. I worked with many Germans who had flown in the war and I was able to recreate his character based on others I knew.

The other German characters in the book were all acquaintances that I encountered in ten years in Germany. They all had their stories to tell. I was not doing research; I mostly just listened, grunted and kept on working.

The one thing that was obvious to me was the magnitude of the war. Civilians heard the distant roar of hundreds of bombers approaching, the scream of the fighters diving and the sound of hundreds of guns firing. As the formations passed overhead, thousands of spent bullets rained down followed by pieces of airplanes and men. After that came foreign men floating down in white parachutes. No one who experienced these things ever forgot them.

After leaving Germany I returned home to Oregon and began working on a ranch. I had briefly met Jim several times before, but now I spent long hours working with him. It was not long before he was telling me all about his experiences in the war. Since he had a willing audience in me, he wanted to make sure that I got all the details right about his missions flying in the Eighth Air Force and his grim time in a German prison.

The Hill

At daybreak, the sun's first rays struck a distant snow-covered mountain, coloring it bright red. As the sun continued to climb, the color of the mountain faded and turned to a softer pink. Now a large lake revealed itself sparkling in the morning light. The morning's quiet was interrupted by ducks and geese nosily feeding. Soon geese started their excited honking as they prepared to fly to another feeding ground.

On a small hill overlooking the lake a young Indian hunter was intently watching a rabbit as it nibbled on the grass. The rabbit was partially hidden by sagebrush. Light dew made the sage sparkle like it was covered in diamonds.

The hunter held a small bow in his hand and slowly drew back the arrow tipped with an obsidian arrowhead. The rabbit slowly moved away from the bush. The young man released the arrow. It flew straight but clipped a branch of the sage brush and flipped over the rabbit. The rabbit was gone in an instant.

The hunter looked in vain for the arrow. It couldn't have disappeared that easily, but it was gone. He was standing on a hill overlooking a large valley. On the horizon the snow-capped mountain had turned pure white with a bright blue sky behind it. Directly below him the lake sparkled in the bright sunlight.

Dejected, the young hunter turned to walk home. He had watched the arrow-maker carefully chip away at the obsidian to make the small arrowhead. His father would be angry; not only had he missed the rabbit but he had also lost the arrow.

The waterfowl went quiet as the birds finished eating and preened themselves or slept with their head tucked under a wing. In the distance, the hunter heard the foreign sound of wagon wheels moaning as they crawled through the soft sand. The people with the wagons looked tired as they plodded on.

The young hunter looked on in alarm. He knew that his tribe had been ambushing wagon trains entering their territory. The ambush site was always the same place on the lake shore near a small outcropping of rocks. Some settlers had been killed there by young warriors. His tribe enjoyed the plunder they brought home.

Most distressing to the young hunter was the fact that, as more and more settlers arrived, they took over his people's hunting grounds. He had spent his entire young life in this region. He had intently listened to the ancient story-teller as he related his tribe's history and how they had fought the neighboring tribes for their hunting and fishing rights. His tribe considered this land sacred because their ancestors were buried here. His people worshiped their ancestors and thought any intrusion by these strangers into to this land would desecrate it.

In the fall, the women of his tribe picked the wild plums that grew on the hill. Not far from where he stood was a large stone mortar. The women would pulverize the plum pits in the mortar and dry the rest of them in the sun. The Indian began to walk down the hill towards the lake. The women were drying fish. He sensed that life as he knew it would be changing. These strangers in the wagons would bring that about.

Years passed and the lake shore no longer touched the bottom of the hill. Much of the lake had been drained and there were fields instead. Someone built a house, constructed a barn and fenced the fields. Irrigation water could be seen in the fields and grass grew in abundance. Cattle and horses grazed on the lush grass. The Indian women still came to the hill each fall to pick wild plums. The settlers also had discovered that the wild plums were good to eat and climbed the hill to pick them. It was not long before they decided that they could grow the plums in their gardens and did not need to climb the hill to gather the fruit.

The Indian boy had grown up. He didn't need a bow now; he carried a more accurate rifle and he did not have to search for lost arrows. Settlers worked in the fields cutting grass for hay to feed their livestock in the winter. The Indian shook his head and laughed at the antics of those crazy men who worked so hard in the hot sun; but how did they eat so well? They had very little time to hunt and fish. Their women did not wander over the land looking for roots and berries. They could be seen working on small plots of land, growing things to eat.

His people spent many leisure hours talking about and worshiping their an-cestors. They stared in stony silence as they watched the settlers build a wooden building larger than their homes. Except for a white cross on the top it looked just like all the other houses. Once a week people would come from all over the valley and enter this building. If you listened carefully, you could hear someone speaking. Later on you could hear singing. Sometimes people would bring food into the building. Was it for a sacrifice?

The settlers had chosen a small plot of land to bury their dead. At times people visited the grave sites and placed flowers by the graves, but that was all.

As time passed the view from the hill slowly changed. The snow-capped mountain still gleamed in all its splendor in the bright sunlight. Roads had been constructed. Newer and better houses were built, and you could see something that resembled wagons, moving without any animals pulling them, on newly built roads.

On the land below the hill, the next generation of settlers built fences and corrals, and the sounds of children playing rang from the hill.

Jim, American cowboy

Many years later, a young cowboy rode to the top of the hill to survey the land below. He was searching for cattle that had strayed from the ranch he worked. He felt good; the beautiful view from the hill and of the green valley below was exhilarating. Thousands of geese filled the sky as they gathered to fly north. He had spent all winter braiding a horse-hair bridle for his horse and he sat quietly admiring it for a moment before looking for cattle tracks in the sandy ground.

He spotted an obsidian arrowhead partially covered with sand. There were arrowheads everywhere you looked, and the cowboy didn't even bother to pick it up. It was only a small one and he could find a bigger one anywhere!

He watched a large flock of geese form up in a V formation. Suddenly an eagle dove down and attacked the geese. It struck one goose and flew away with it dangling from his talons. The formation scattered but then reformed quickly and closed the gap made by the lost goose.

Jim urged his horse forward. Little did he know that one day he would associate the eagle attack with the German fighters attacking the American bomber formations.

There was no sign of the lost cattle. The day was getting warmer and Jim decided to head for home. The bright blue sky so common in that region was slowly being invaded by dark war clouds on the Western horizon. As he approached the ranch he could see the owner waiting for him. He greeted Jim but was looking down as he absently dragged his boot back and forth across the soft ground. Without looking up, he asked if Jim had found the lost cattle.

"Nope," was Jim's quiet reply, as he loosened the cinch on his saddle.

The boss scratched the stubble on his chin. Without looking up he said, "I guess you know there is talk of war in Europe."

Jim answered, "Yep that's what I hear. Hitler is already sending airplanes into Spain to fight the Communists."

The boss looked up at Jim and remarked, "You are my top hand and I would sure hate to lose you. They are going to take lots of young men to fight in the war. I am sure we are going to be short of help when the fighting starts. Since you are older than most of my help, I hear tell that employers can get exceptions for certain people if they need them badly enough."

Jim lifted his saddle off the horse and started to carry it to the tack room. He had not given much thought to what he would do if America would get involved in a war, but he somehow felt insulted at the thought that he would not fight if he was needed. He gave his boss an angry look. "I will fight if I am called," he proudly announced.

Emil, German pilot

While Jim was trying to understand what war might bring, a young German was lining up his airplane to take pictures of a burning Spanish village. Emil was trying to find a gap between the billows of smoke where he could get a clear shot of the damage. His wing tilted up and he saw the dark circle with a white X of the Spanish Nationalist insignia on it.

As the nose of the airplane touched the outskirts of the burning village, he curtly spoke to the photographer, "*Kamera einschalten.*"

"*Yawohl,*" answered a very nervous young man on his first combat mission.

Emil held the airplane perfectly level and at exactly the proper altitude. He could not avoid seeing the dead bodies lying on the ground. His airplane flew through the swirling smoke and he smelled burning flesh. Until now the war had been only a game with new and exciting toys to play with, but at that moment the reality of it struck with full force.

It didn't help when the photographer ask innocently, "*Was stinkt denn da?*" (what's that awful smell?) Now he understood what the training and indoctrination was all about.

Emil's life in Germany had not been easy. The economy had been a disaster during his younger years, and people had no hope of it improving. Still, his schooling was excellent and his grades had been very good.

The question on all the students' minds was, "Will there be any jobs for us when we graduate?" Then Hitler arrived on the scene. Many Germans did not like him, but he did revive their economy. Little did they know that they were like cattle in a feed lot enjoying the good times, unaware that the next trip would be to the slaughterhouse.

Emil's life changed abruptly. Before he knew it, he was training to be a pilot. His grasp of technology and good reflexes meant that he left many of his classmates behind. His lack of interest in politics was noted by the political officers on the staff. They thought that he could be very useful to the Nazi cause, but he was not going to be officer material.

He trained as a fighter pilot, but because of his interest in photography was cross-trained as reconnaissance pilot. Now he was involved in the actual fighting, there was no one he could speak to about his experiences, because he was afraid of being reported to the Nazi party officer.

Earlier, one of the older World War One veterans told him how he had hardened himself to the things that he had seen and done. Emil had not given this information any attention at the time, because he was having such a good time learning to fly. He had volunteered to fly in Spain because he thought it would provide some more good training. Now he would need to start this mind-hardening process, *aber schnell*! (fast).

Right now he was flying a photo airplane taking pictures without a fighter escort. The Luftwaffe was just now transitioning to its new Messerschmidt fighter, and he would have to deal with any Spanish Republican fighters on his own.

He now began a lifelong habit, called 'rubbernecking' by American pilots. He ordered his co-pilot to watch all the time, and his machine gunner to report all air traffic. After a nerve-wracking return trip, he spotted several old biplanes circling his home base. He knew the familiar silhouette and that they were fellow Germans. Now all he had to worry about was the strong crosswind blowing across the runway.

If Emil's conscience was bothering him, a Spanish nationalist staff officer had no such qualms. When asked by a German officer why he wanted to bomb Spanish towns, he shrugged and said, "We bomb it and bomb it, and *bueno*, why not?"

Emil walked back to the building where he was living, exhausted and craving sleep. Before he could lay down, his roommate excitedly barged in.

"I had a great day! I put a few rounds into a Republican fighter and he crash-landed in a field. Now the officers will have to accept me as an equal."

The roommate was a *Feldwebel* (sergeant) like Emil and like Emil, would stay that way because of his political views. Despite Emil's protests that he wasn't hungry, his roommate begged him to come and eat with him.

On their way to eat, they walked by the officers' dining room. A group of officers were discussing the day's fighting and how they needed to change the makeup of their formations. Werner, a handsome young *Leutnant* with dark hair and a neat mustache resembling Clark Gable, his Luftwaffe hat jauntily tipped on his head, gave Emil a loud greeting.

"Good work. I hear you got some good pictures."

Emil had trained with Werner on fighters and knew him very well. He remarked "I see you are still flying the slow old *Heinkel 51* biplane. If you can work your way up to an *Me-109* you might catch my photo machine."

The officer pilots grudgingly nodded a greeting to Emil's roommate. They had seen him shoot down the Republican fighter. After Werner became a general, Emil would still be a *Feldwebel*, though a very deadly and experienced one.

Jim

On the ranch, Jim's life continued in the same pattern it had always followed. He put his conversation with his boss in the back of his mind. Most of the people he worked with had simply refused to think about the prospect of a war. When Jim heard that the Nazis had invaded Poland, he was certain that this war would change his life, probably forever. It was September when he heard about the invasion. He decided to do more hunting this fall to hone up his shooting skills—he might be needing them soon.

Werner, German pilot

Meanwhile the handsome Werner had written reports about his flying in Spain and the role of airplanes in supporting the Army's ground forces. That kept him flying the *Henshel 123,* another old biplane instead of the modern *Me-109.*

Now he was a *Hauptmann* (Captain), teaching the next generation of Luftwaffe pilots ground support tactics. Not only was he flying obsolete airplanes, but the cockpit was open and even on a warm day the pilot himself was seldom warm.

Jim

During September, Jim had time for some hunting and fishing with friends. In the back of everyone's mind was the gathering of black war clouds. It had frightened everyone when Hitler's armies had defeated the Poles in just a few weeks. All the young men were asking themselves, "Where will I be next year at this time?"

Jim had put saddle soap on the horse's harness and greased the wheel bearing on the hay wagon. Now he was forking hay over the side of the wagon to the waiting cattle below.

The work horses plodded slowly ahead. If Jim wanted them to change their course he needed only to shout out either, "gee" or "haw" and they would turn either left or right. He was proud of the fact that he could even get the horses to back the wagon into the barn with only voice commands.

Hans, German Unteroffizier

The winter weather allowed the Luftwaffe to build its strength. Newly trained pilots like *Unteroffizier* (Corporal) Hans, who had just received his pilot's wings, were assigned to a *Staffel* (squadron) that flew the newer *Me-109*.

The older pilots who had flown the *Alten Kisten* (old crates) were jealous that youngsters just out of training were assigned to fly the new planes. They did not make the lives of the beginners easy. In spite of this the new pilots picked up some valuable training.

Hans was worried that the war might never start again and he would not get to use his new skills. The older pilots advised him to enjoy his *Urlaub* (vacation), as he would soon get more excitement than he wanted.

Hans had always been a loner in school, mischievous and rebelling against the strict discipline in the German schools. He still managed to receive a good education. When he entered the German army, he had scored well enough on his tests to be chosen for pilot training. He hated the classroom work but his flying was good enough to pass the course. Because he was always in trouble with the political officer, it was decided by his superiors that he would probably never rise above the rank of *Unteroffizier*, but if handled correctly he could be useful to the cause.

Emil, German pilot

Hitler could not wait until he controlled all of Europe. Only the German general staff—and later the weather—could slow him down. Now every available photographic airplane was flying when possible. Aerial photography in itself was never very exciting. Now, flying almost the same area every day had Emil hoping for a transfer back to fighter command. The only problem was that the fighters were flying even less.

Emil was getting increasingly bored with the constant flying over the same territory. He had access to enough information to know that as soon as the countryside dried out, Hitler was going to attack. But it wasn't until May that Hitler was able to invade France, Belgium and Holland.

Emil was suddenly busy taking aerial photos ahead of the advancing German army. The advance was so fast that sometimes, by the time the photos were developed, the ground forces were already past that point!

Despite perfect planning of the attack, there were many costly mistakes. The Nazis quickly covered them up and they would not be revealed until many years after the war.

Three *Heinkel* bombers bound for an airfield at Dijon far south of Paris, instead bombed Freiburg, a German town fifteen miles inside Germany! That mistake killed sixty Germans.

The lead navigator in the next group of bombers realized what had happened and radioed Luftwaffe Headquarters. "*Drei Luftwaffe Flugzeuge haben die Bomben auf Freiburg abgeworfen!*"

There was a long silence and then a very official voice loudly proclaimed, "*Unmöglich!*" (impossible) After they landed, the crew were told not to talk about this to anyone. The Nazi high command just blamed it on the *Engländer. Kein Problemo*!

Werner, newly promoted major

After many years of flying the *Alten Kisten* in Spain and later in Poland, Werner finally got his chance to fly a modern fighter. Now he would not have to put up with the unspoken ridicule of *Feldwebels* like Emil who were getting to fly all the newer airplanes.

The *Me-109* fit Werner's personality perfectly. During the invasion of France, he came upon Royal Air Force Hurricanes and attacking from behind, was able to shoot down three of them. After all these years of preparation he finally was able to attack someone who could fight back. He shot down all three before they could fire back at him.

He had expected to be elated. Instead he had a bad taste in his mouth and fought back a twinge of conscience. Even after he had landed and received the congratulations of his comrades, he started to have some doubts about the war he was fighting.

Hans

Hans at last was getting to fly in combat. What he hadn't anticipated was being so frightened in the air. He felt lucky if he could stay with his leader. His flight did not encounter any opposition, but after landing he was shaking so badly that he thought he might be sick.

The mechanics saw his white and sweaty face and politely looked away. Later they would joke about the frightened Luftwaffe Eagle who had almost died of fright on his first mission!

Jim

J im was busy in May 1940. He finally had finished the tedious, twice-daily
cattle feeding that had occupied him all winter. Now the fields were green
with new grass. The hay wagon was parked for a few months and the work horses would start plowing in much warmer weather.

Jim had heard about the Nazi invasion of France. No one was surprised
about that, but everyone was stunned by how quickly the French were defeated.
The First World War had taken place in the same areas and had resulted in four
years of fighting. This time it had taken only a few weeks.

The seed was planted in everyone's mind that the Luftwaffe and Wehrmacht (German Army) were invincible. Hitler was certain that they were! Victory
had closed the Nazi mind to reality. They did not care to notice that the countries they had invaded were in fact militarily and morally weak.

Meanwhile Jim was getting ready to mow hay. He liked getting the mower
ready to cut hay. He replaced old or worn sections on the mower bar and made
sure everything was greased and oiled.

Emil

E mil was flying over Dunkirk. The smoke rose high in the sky and obscured most of the ground. Through the breaks in the smoke he could see the masses of English troops standing on the beach. He had orders to take pictures of the Dunkirk beachhead. He was certain that he was wasting film but lined up and leveled out. He wanted everything to be perfect, because he knew that the Nazis in his unit were watching his every move.

He had just called out, "*Kamera einshalten*," when someone on the radio screamed, "*Spitfeurs*"! Emil's plane shuddered and he saw pieces of metal flying off his wing.

Two Spitfires passed over his airplane and disappeared into the smoke. Right behind them were two *Me-109s*. Wisps of smoke streamed from the lead 109's wings as he fired at the Spitfires.

Emil told the photographer to keep taking pictures, so no one could accuse him of not carrying out his mission. As he was turning back to his base a familiar voice called out over the radio: "*Horrido!*" the Luftwaffe cry for victory.

Emil suddenly realized how dangerous this aerial game of war was going to be. His time in Spain had had just enough danger to make it interesting. The Polish campaign was more brutal but not that dangerous. The French war had moved so fast that they did not have enough fighters to bother with photo airplanes.

Now, as the Luftwaffe came in range of English fighters, the war was suddenly more difficult and dangerous. Emil realized that he would need to be more alert and watchful than he thought possible.

He lowered the landing gear prior to landing at his airfield. He could see two *Me-109's* that had just landed, coming to a stop before the operations building. Emil stopped next to them. He noticed that the gun patches that normally covered the cannon barrels were shot off and he could see traces of smoke on the wings.

A smiling Werner standing next to one of them remarked, "You should be happy that I finally got a good fighter, now I can really protect you. You should be more careful watching your tail, or, better still, get an *Me-109* to take your pictures with."

Emil noticed the cartoon character on Werner's fighter and remarked, "I hope this war remains a comedy for all of us."

Jim

At the same time that Emil and Werner were fighting English Spitfires and thousands of English and French Soldiers were waiting to be evacuated from Dunkirk, Jim was irrigating fields of alfalfa and grass. The weather was warm and clear, memories of the long winter were fading fast and normally Jim would be looking forward to a warm and pleasant summer.

The news of the war in Europe was bad. France was defeated, and it looked like England was not going to survive either. The war was always in the background of peoples' minds. The clouds drew closer, growing larger and darker.

Of course, everyone hoped it would not affect them that much. But young men knew that if America went to war, they would be the ones doing the fighting. Jim didn't know it then, but he had two years of peace before he would be on his way to war.

Hans

The young *Unteroffizier* Hans was gaining experience and confidence quickly. The older pilots were still nervous about having a novice flying on their wing, but Hans was more confident now. Fortunately, he only saw a few enemy aircraft and these from a distance. He was not the only beginner flying with the Luftwaffe.

Kurt, German Leutnant

Nineteen-year-old Kurt had just finished his training and was struggling to control the *Me-109*. Landing and take-offs were exciting. The narrow landing gear plus a huge engine made the airplane want to swing violently to the left. The *Schwarzemänner* (mechanics) were instructed to keep the left landing gear strut at a higher air pressure than the right landing gear. Done properly it made the airplane tip to the right when sitting on the ground.

Experienced pilots could tell from a distance if it had been done. Nervous beginners would sometimes forget to check, a pile of broken airplanes attesting to that.

Kurt loved to fly and worked hard to master the difficult *Me-109*. Some of the airfields had a grass runway next to the main one. Kurt liked the grass better than the hard surface. The older pilots did not like to fly with the beginners, but taught them how to survive by stating, "Just stay on my wing and don't get lost."

Werner

Werner started to pick up victories in the air. He finished off two old British bombers. Since the gunners in the bombers fired back at him he felt it had been a fair fight. The battle against the Royal Air Force was not as easy now as the previous ones. The pilots were well-trained, they had good fighters, and there were enough of them to put up a desperate fight.

The *Me-109* was as good as the English fighters but couldn't carry enough fuel to stay over England very long. The short wars in Poland and France had convinced Hitler that he could make short work of England as well. When the losses in airplanes and crews mounted, the smooth operations of the Luftwaffe became disorganized. Now *der Dicke* (Goering, the fat one) noticed that the flamboyant Werner had become a decorated ace.

Jim

J im's work became less demanding as autumn approached. The news from England was not as bad as had expected. The Germans were still bombing London but they had already withdrawn their invasion force and were looking eastward toward Russia.

Jim was living like most Americans, with one eye on the war news while going about his normal life. Most of the young men were trying to ignore the news, because none of them could imagine where they would go or what they would do in a war.

There were times after a difficult day that Jim wished someone would take him away from this hard, boring life and let him do something more exciting. He tried to imagine what he might end up doing in the army. He was good with horses, but not many horses were needed in a modern war.

He hoped that he might be trained as a mechanic. There were many machines being used right now. He had heard that it was possible for some men to be trained as aircraft mechanics. That sounded interesting, but he didn't think there was much chance of that happening to an older ranch hand. He was over thirty and hoped he wouldn't end up in the infantry; surely he was too old for that.

Emil

E mil was now busy taking pictures of the English coast. He flew one of the latest *Me-109s*. It had a pressurized cockpit that allowed it to fly at an altitude of over forty thousand feet. Since he was flying so close to enemy territory he had another *Me-109* as an escort.

Emil would reach his altitude, level off, and start taking pictures, his wing man staying behind him. The English also had special Spitfires equipped to fly at high altitude. The Spitfires could not reach the level of the Germans but they would trail the *Me-109s*, waiting for the Germans to make a sharp turn and lose some altitude so they could get a shot at them. Emil had given strict orders to his wing man to follow his every move and not even think about the *Engländer* behind them.

Emil had a strict routine that he always followed. He would take off before breakfast since he did not want a full stomach removing any oxygen from his brain at that altitude. When he landed he always had time to enjoy his breakfast break. The German *Frühstückspause* was the great moment of the day.

One morning before takeoff, Emil received an unpleasant surprise. His usual wing man was not there, and he was greeted instead by a very young fighter pilot. Emil did not want someone so inexperienced protecting him over enemy territory. Emil realized that the young man was not listening when he explained why he must not transmit on the radio.

Emil tried to emphasize the need for maintaining his position. "You are not to engage the Spitfires that will be following us. If you turn too fast you will stall and fall out of position. Then you are a dead man for sure."

The young pilot grinned, clearly thinking, "This man is too old and cautious to be flying in a real war."

The English radar could always pickup Emil's signal long before he arrived. The Luftwaffe knew how important those pictures were for the planned invasion, so they had fighters standing by to protect Emil and his wing man.

Emil's new *Mr-109* had water and methanol alcohol injected into the cylinders so it quickly climbed to altitude.

29

Emil's wing man was flying the new model *Me-109 G* for the first time, so he excitedly transmitted to both friend and foe, *"Der Gustaf ist eine tolle Maschine."* (this Gustav model is one great machine).

Emil could only shake his head and silently wonder how he got this *dummer Kerl* for this important mission. Emil had leveled his airplane and was flying right on course, when the young wingman screamed *"Spitfeuer!"*

He had been told explicitly before the mission not to break radio silence for any reason. He was not to worry about the English fighters as they could not fly high enough to bother the *Gustafs*.

Emil was worried that this mission might not turn out that well. His stomach was telling him that it was impatiently waiting for *Frühstück*. He didn't hear from his wing man for a long time. He was hoping that he was trailing behind like he had been told to do.

Suddenly his wingman shouted, "Enough of this, I am going to get me an *Engländer.*"

Emil heard an explosion in the distance and with a sigh, turned off the camera and turned towards Germany. Below, he saw a *Gustaf* spinning before it hit the water, his wingman swinging slowly in his parachute above.

Emil was irritated that this idiot had spoiled a perfectly good photo mission. Reluctantly, he radioed the German search and rescue boats to pick up the young pilot. The English fighters were already circling the German pilot in the water. They should have been watching their backs.

Just a few moments later one of the Spitfires splashed down into the water, shot down by a *Me-109* followed by a steady stream of German fighters. From the north came more Spitfires and another *Me-109* hit the water.

Emil stayed on his perch high above the melee, giving the German command a running commentary about the battle. By the time the battle was over, Emil was sure that seven *Me-109s* were lost and at least that many Spitfires had crashed into the sea. Both the English and German rescue boats headed home.

Emil's stomach was rumbling, *"Verdammt noche 'mal,* I am going to miss my *Frühstückspause,"* he thought as he returned to where he had stopped filming before and started his camera again.

The English radar picked up his signal and sent a message to command headquarters. "That bloody Hun is still up there taking pictures!"

Headquarters replied with a sigh, "We do not have any fighter available that can fly that high."

Emil finished his mission and landed at his home airfield. Airmen arrived to remove the camera from his plane.

His commanding officer greeted him when he entered the ready room with, "What took you so long? You should have landed an hour ago."

Emil, thinking about his stomach replied, "I missed my *Frühstück*." Years after the war whenever Emil would tell the story, he always emphasized that some *Dummkopf* had caused him to miss his breakfast! He let someone else talk about the missing wingman and the major air battle. He had finished his mission and had the pictures to prove it.

Young German pilots

The younger pilots like *Unteroffizier* Hans and *Leutnant* Kurt were quickly gaining in experience and confidence.

Hans had once thought he was indestructible. On one of his first missions over England a very impolite Spitfire pilot had put a string of bullets into his wing, only a meter away from his body. That made him both frightened and angry. The fear would soon harden his conscience; the anger would remain.

When Kurt saw his first German aircraft go spiraling down in flames he wondered, "This is so dangerous; how can I survive this?" He immediately began to ask the more experienced pilots what tactics they used in combat. Some were very sullen and did not want to talk about fighting. They were content to let him learn it the hard way believing, *no one ever helped me.*

Kurt quickly understood that these men had never really thought about what they were doing and didn't care about learning more. They were just trusting in their luck to get them through the war. He was determined to study aerial combat and learn all he could about it. He did learn the hard way and was wounded so many times that he had plenty of time to think about his mistakes in a hospital bed.

Neither Hans nor Kurt would shoot down any airplanes in the Battle of Britain, but it gave them enough experience to get to the next stage.

Werner

Werner had been promoted very quickly as the war progressed and was soon ordered to supreme headquarters to be given a high award by Goering. The fat one praised the pilots for their bravery. In his next breath he told them that he was not happy with the Luftwaffe's role in the battle of Britain and he placed much of the blame on the fighter pilots.

This infuriated Werner. Many of his friends had lost their lives in that battle. Werner, his dark eyes flaming with indignation and anger, sarcastically reminded Goering that the pilots were equipped with airplanes that did not have enough range to fight very long over England.

The fat one quietly asked Werner what kind of fighter he wanted. He loudly exclaimed, "Some English Spitfires!"

A stunned Goering left the room. A shocked group of staff officers exited swiftly, not wanting to witness an execution.

When Werner passed through some of the larger towns on his way back to his unit, he was shocked at the behavior of the civilian population. They hardly seemed aware that a war was going on. They had good, easy lives and knew that some of the good food and wine came from conquered countries.

Had someone been killed fighting for them? Yes there had been a few young men who never came back, but it was necessary for some of the slower ones to die for their country. The civilians were afraid to ask why Werner was wearing one of the highest order of Iron Crosses at his throat. They were as much afraid of their own military as they were of their enemies. Coming from the intensity of war and then seeing the indifference of the German population caused Werner to hate his own people as much as the enemy he had been fighting.

Jim

Jim had enjoyed the nice fall air and done some waterfowl hunting while the Battle of Britain raged on. He was always surprised at how easy it was for him to shoot birds out of the air. Of course he had years of experience using a shotgun

He could never have imagined that he would need that skill in fighting men with several years of combat experience and who were presently gaining more skills. Now all he had to do was get through another winter of feeding cows and helping with the calving. He couldn't shake the feeling that his life would change dramatically in the not too distant future. Even people who were not interested in world events were feeling uneasy.

Emil

E mil had an easy winter, with only a few flights along the Polish border with Russia. The weather was terrible and Emil was certain that spring would bring plenty of action as the weather improved.

He was already doing fewer photo flights and more reconnaissance flights. He did not need to fly a perfect heading and altitude, but he was disappointed since any *Dummkopf* able to read a map could fly a reconnaissance flight.

As the weather improved he flew over the North Sea, watching for English ships and reporting immediately any that he saw. One morning he was given a briefing by a higher ranking officer. He was told that the English battleship *Hood* was steaming out to engage the German battleship *Bismarck*.

Emil received the frequencies that he needed to communicate with the German ship, and given the location of the *Hood*. He was told that his airplane was fueled to the maximum and he should take off immediately to report the location of the enemy.

Emil was alarmed. He had gotten into a daily routine and even though there was danger involved he had become hardened to it. This was something else! The *Hood* was one of the largest battleships ever built and the pride of the Royal Navy.

Emil had a radio operator to help with the communications and two machine gunners to protect him. As he leveled off over the raging ocean, he thought it humorous that he might be attacking a battleship with two light machine guns.

His crew members had been briefed on their mission, during a long flight over water, Emil was not surprised when the nose gunner called out, "*Mein Gott, da ist ein riesen Schiff direkt vor uns.*" (There is a giant ship right in front of us.)

Emil didn't need to ask the name of the ship. Tracer bullets reached out and almost enveloped his airplane. Emil applied full power to both engines and climbed into the low-hanging clouds.

Even as they flew into the clouds, tracer bullets kept streaking past his airplane. Emil shouted to the stunned radio operator to tell the *Bismarck* that they had found the *Hood*. The *Bismarck* wanted a continuous account of the *Hood's* location.

Emil's problem was that every time he came down out of the clouds, the *Hood* opened fire. He tried to keep a greater distance, but then she would fire a larger gun at him, trying to splash him with a one ton shell that threw water as high as his airplane.

He was thankful now that he had taken off with a full tank of fuel. The *Bismarck* was racing toward the *Hood* but from Emil's view it appeared it would be hours before the two would meet.

Now he had a routine established. Dive out of the cloud, spot the *Hood*, climb back into the cloud, radio the *Bismarck* the *Hood's* position, fly for a few minutes and appear from a different location as he dove out of the clouds.

Emil had been shot at before, but this routine was getting tiring. This was a major battle and he did not like the spot he was in because he had little or no control over his situation. He was nervous and shouted at the radio operator.

When one of the gunners became airsick he felt betrayed. He should have been given more experienced crew members. His throat was dry and he was weak from hunger.

After several hours of patrolling, he finally caught sight of the *Bismarck* speeding towards the *Hood*. When he radioed the *Bismarck*, he received the order to keep the *Hood* in sight at all times

He gave the *Bismarck* its distance to the *Hood* and flew back into the clouds. Next time he came out he spotted the smoke of the *Bismarck's* guns firing on the *Hood*.

Emil stayed out of the cloud long enough to see four splashes—two on each side of the *Hood*. He radioed the *Bismarck* to fire for effect.

The *Hood* threw a final round at him as he pulled back into the clouds. He spent a few minutes in the cloud and slowly dropped out to see what had happened. At first, he was disoriented and thought he had flown in the wrong direction. Where the *Hood* had been a few minutes before, there was nothing!

Her escort ship was still there firing at the *Bismarck*. The airsick nose gunner yelled that he could see what looked like the bottom of a ship.

Sure enough, during the time Emil been in the cloud the *Bismarck* had fired on the Hood, hitting the ammunition hold. She had blown up and sank, taking fifteen hundred English sailors with her!

In stunned silence, Emil and his crew tried to grasp what they had just seen. Quietly, Emil radioed the *Bismarck* for permission to return to base. The *Bismarck* radioed back, "*Dankeschön.* Go home."

Emil dropped down and flew just over the tops of the waves, rocking his wings at the cheering sailors on the deck of the *Bismarck* waving at him. Many of them had only three days to live before they would share the fate of the English sailors on the *Hood*.

Jim

Jim and the American people around him could not imagine the magnitude of the war in Europe. He heard about the thousands of people involved and the great number of tanks and airplanes. But in his wildest imagination he could not relate it to anything he had ever seen.

People who were closer to the war wanted to stay out of it. People with large established factories could not wait to get involved in the war. The American president could not see any way to avoid it. When Jim heard about the invasion of Russia he realized that total war was not far away and he would be involved.

Kurt

As young Luftwaffe lieutenant, Kurt knew he should be excited about a new war in which to prove himself. The combat in England had given him more flying experience, but the losses in pilots and the sight of those more experienced than him dying in combat left him with an empty feeling.

Shooting down two Russian airplanes in his first days in Russia helped build his confidence. He was congratulated by his comrades, but all the combat pilots knew that this was going to be a long, hard war.

Kurt continued to have concerns about the justification for this war. He tried to hide his real doubts with his aggressiveness in combat. He managed to shoot down ten more Russians in the next month, and his fellow pilots wondered how this mild, pleasant man on the ground could become a wild man in aerial combat.

The payback came swiftly when a Russian shot him down and put him in the hospital for three months. That at least took him out of the harsh conditions on the Russian front.

Kurt had a lot of time to think when he was in the hospital bed. He decided that he did not like to kill people. He also understood that, if he tried to stop flying, he would be signing his own death warrant. After much contemplation he decided that he wanted to keep using his natural outgoing personality to encourage his fellow pilots.

He would try his best to study the different combat situations and find solutions to the problems that the Luftwaffe was facing. He hoped that he could impress the Nazi goons who were watching his every move, but not become a Nazi, retain his own character and survive the war intact.

Werner

Werner thought someone had dropped a bomb on him. He heard that his best friend and his commander had been killed in an air crash. Then a beaming Goering had flown to his base with the information that Werner had been picked to be general in charge of all German fighter aircraft.

The last thing he wanted was a desk job. He was not yet thirty and knew he was very good at flying and leading. Why would anyone want to sit at desk instead of flying a fighter? But there was no way that he could say no to *der Dicke*. He was sickened by the thought he would be leaving his friends in his *Gruppe* and he would be working with Goering with no one between them. Not a bright future.

Werner had always been very outspoken in dealing with his superiors. He had also gone his separate way in dealing with military regulations. He realized that Hitler and Goering knew the war was going badly. They were aware that the only men capable of winning the war were men who would stand up to them.

Werner was determined to survive both the war and the Nazi regime. He would stand up to Goering and fight the enemy with all his strength. He was not only fighting the allies who were getting stronger, but he would need to fight his own leaders.

Hans

Unteroffizier Hans was relieved to not be involved in the invasion of Russia. He had seen enough of the war to realize that it would not be ending soon and he had better enjoy the life he had right now. The English were sending over enough fighters to give him some flying time but nothing as intense as the Battle of Britain.

Emil

Emil was not as fortunate since his flying skills were needed in the desert. He was sent to Libya. He now flew a *Me-110*, a twin engine airplane, most of the time without an escort.

He did have a rear-facing machine gunner and Emil was always reminding him to keep watching for enemy aircraft. It was difficult to do when the landscape was nothing but sand and more sand.

Even if the gunner was not afraid of the enemy he would stay awake knowing the trouble he would be in if he ever fell asleep on a flight with Emil. The English did not have the radar systems in the desert that they had in England so Emil did not need to worry about English fighters as much.

Still, the heat and living conditions were horrible. The food was bad and full of sand. The water was limited to drinking only. The only time he could bathe was when he found a beach to swim in in the Gulf of Sirte.

He soon learned to make a reconnaissance flight over the ocean opposite the beach where he wanted to swim. The Gulf of Sirte was full of sunken ships from the recent fighting. They tended to leak oil, ruining the beach for swimming.

He managed to find the clear spots on the beach, so there were times when he could relax and forget the war and it dangers. When he didn't want to swim anymore, he searched for Roman artifacts lying on the beach. He would study them for a time before throwing them back into the water. He had no place for artifacts in his airplane. He needed all that space and weight for fuel.

Jim

J im was still working on the ranch, though he had known for some time that
his life was going to be changing soon. Still, it was a great shock when Pearl
Harbor was attacked. No one had been sure how America was going to enter
the war.

The American government had expected the war in Europe to escalate to
the point where they would have to enter the conflict. Now the Americans had
been blind-sided by a Japanese sneak attack.

When the American Congress declared war on the Japanese, Hitler gleefully declared war on the Americans. The German military was appalled by this
stupidity. They were fighting in Russia and woefully short of men and equipment there.

They were also fighting in a vast desert that swallowed up men and supplies
at an ever-increasing rate. Hitler no longer thought of himself as a human but
was beginning to see himself as almost a god. All those numbers were just propaganda from the Americans. Surely no one had that many resources available.

Werner

Werner sat in his office in stunned silence. He knew he had the best pilots in the world. The trouble was, the Luftwaffe was not training enough pilots to even replace their losses in England. His fighters were devastating the Russian air force but still taking losses that couldn't be replaced.

Werner may not have been a religious man, but he was still using the logic of his Protestant ancestors. He could see reality and the numbers were not on Germany's side.

Jim

Jim knew that the younger men he worked with did not have the slightest idea of what their future held. Not many were looking forward to it. They were afraid that it would be necessary to defeat at least two different nations, one of which had terrorized some of Europe's great armies and now raced across Russia with what American media called a blitz.

The German general in North Africa was making English Generals look like amateurs. The Japanese Navy had destroyed much of the American Navy at Pearl Harbor with hardly any resistance.

A stunned military bureaucracy was suddenly faced with the fact that the Japanese Navy was the best-equipped and trained in the world. The admiral responsible for building this great fleet had been educated in a Protestant missionary school. He was not following the ancient, suicidal Samurai code.

He planned and trained much like the Americans did. The American naval planners had closed their minds to what was going on in Japan. How could this backward nation have advanced so quickly in just a few years?

Jim had not finished High School, but like many of his age still had a good education. He could read well and was the sort of person who could survive and innovate in any difficult situation.

The military planners understood that there were millions of men and women capable of learning skills and building machines in a few short months that could win a modern war.

American factories began expanding and planning for a big surge in orders. Airplanes that had been planned but never built were suddenly put into production, though most were already obsolete before they were built.

Both German and Japanese airplanes were more modern and faster. Their pilots were already trained and had years of experience. Americans were scrambling to put flying schools together. Anyone with any civilian flying experience was put into the training system to start immediately training others. Sometimes they had to find their own lodging and food.

Streams of civilians headed towards factories, where they would be working and building war materiel within weeks of their arrival. A society that had just begun to move into the industrial age had overnight changed so rapidly that most people never knew what happened.

A Japanese admiral had warned his government that if they started a war with the Americans, they would awaken a sleeping giant that would eventually destroy them. Within a few months the American would already be fighting back.

Most Americans realized that life as they knew it before Pearl Harbor would never return, and those who received well-paying jobs were happy if they never returned to the old life.

One cold morning as Jim was tightening the cinch on his saddle, his boss approached him, patted Jim's horse on his neck, deliberately straightening some strands of hair on the horse's mane.

After a few more moments of silence he quietly spoke. "I hear tell that you're thinking about volunteering for the Army. That would really put me in a bind. You are the only competent hired help I have. It would sure be a shame if you got killed or badly hurt. If you stay with me on the ranch I'll give you a good raise. Surely there are enough of these young fellows to fight the war."

It was beyond Jim's comprehension that his boss did not realize how serious the consequences would be if America lost this war. Did he think he could win this war by raising more beef? Jim was volunteering to lay his life down to turn back the enemies of his country. This man had access to the same news as Jim had and still did not understand the danger he was in! "I reckon he must have had his head in the sand," Jim reasoned years later.

By now Jim was boiling inside. He hoped that he could control himself. As calmly as he could, he said, "You will have to get by as best you can. Maybe do a lot of the work yourself. I will be leaving soon. Tomorrow I am going to visit my parents and some friends to say goodbye."

With that he pulled his saddle off the horse and took it with him to pick up his possessions from the bunk house. His prize possession had been his braided horse hair bridle, but last winter someone had stolen it when he wasn't watching.

With a sigh he laughed and thought, "I probably won't need a braided bridle where I'm going." Still he would always think of his lost bridle and regret that someone had stolen it. Years later, it was always something that he would talk about when reminiscing about his life working on ranches. It would go down in history with the story of Emil's missed breakfast.

Thinking of his last conversation with his boss, Jim smiled and thought "Why did I stay so long with that outfit?" He actually felt good about starting a new life of adventure. He could not know what kind of excitement he would experience!

A few weeks later, Jim boarded a train with several other men going to the same army reception center. The recruiting sergeant had taken one look at the new recruits and had handed Jim the folder with their enlistment papers. He wanted to be sure that they arrived safely at their destination.

The first hour on the train the young men were excited and looking forward to an adventure in the army. They were still passing through an area that they knew well. They had traveled here with parents and friends.

When they realized that they were leaving all this behind and might never see it again, reality stepped in and they suddenly became quiet and a little afraid. They were going to war! This adventure had become something that they had not been prepared for.

The long trip gave them time to think about their former lives. They smoked a lot and when it came time to eat, many found that they had no appetite. Jim was happy to think about doing something different.

His only worry was that he didn't want to serve in the infantry. He had done enough hard work in his life. He was certain that he was qualified to train as a mechanic but he could not imagine that he might be working and flying in airplanes. When the train reached their destination, they were loaded on a bus and driven to their army base. When the bus stopped and the doors opened they had reached the end of their civilian lives and belonged to their nation's military.

A sergeant rapidly screaming obscenities greeted them as they stepped from the bus. Jim had heard from other men with experience in the army what awaited him, so he was not surprised at his welcome to the army.

Many of the younger men were stunned and had difficulty understanding what was happening to them. The time they had spent wondering about their future was over and they did not have time to think about anything further. All they needed to do was to obey the sergeant's orders and do it right away.

They stood in stunned silence as new clothing and boots were thrown at them. They watched as other recruits were given haircuts, touched their own hair and bade it farewell. They were marched from one building to another while being harassed by the cadre, called names, and humiliated for not understanding an order.

For those who thought that they were heroes for enlisting it was understandably humbling. Most were too stunned to protest. They were too cowed to even try for fear of being ridiculed by the other recruits.

After receiving many injections for diseases they never knew existed, they were finally brought into a large auditorium. A young lieutenant trying to sound as authoritarian as possible, explained in a squeaky voice that they would find a large envelope on their seat.

In it they would find their orders telling them what they were going to be trained for. Those going to the infantry let out loud moans.

Jim could not believe his eyes: he was going to the Army Air Corp! As he read more carefully he saw the word mechanic; at least he wasn't going to be in the infantry. The man next to him asked where he was going.

When Jim told him the man exclaimed, "Some people have all the luck. You may not even have to go overseas."

Jim drawled, "I'll go where they send me."

After that, Jim took the next train headed south. He enjoyed the mountains and green trees of Washington and Oregon. When the train was half way through California he was already tired of the long trip. He had never given much thought to where Texas lay in relation to Washington state.

Now the scenery was changing. Oak trees replaced the green firs and pines. The trees were green, but the grass around them was already turning brown and the temperature climbed dramatically.

Werner

As Jim was heading for Texas and the beginning of his training, the German army began its spring offensive in Russia. Massive attacks pushed the Russians backward. But it was not like the first year of the war, when the Russian army had simply given up without a fight. Now they were fighting back. The Germans were still advancing but taking many more causalities.

Werner sat in his office staring out the window. Below him he could see rows of German fighters. The crazy camouflage colors with the black cross on the airplanes created a sinister picture. Werner laughed to himself as he thought, "if I didn't know they were on my side I would be frightened."

He had just received a phone call from Goering. The fat one was in a bad mood. He had just read the most recent report that Werner had sent him.

"You know that Hitler does not want to hear any more negative reports about the strength of the *Amis*." Goering complained. "He says that is all Roosevelt propaganda. No sane person could believe those numbers. It is *streng verboten* (strictly forbidden) to send any more reports about the *Amis'* production numbers."

Werner answered, "*Jawohl*," and slammed the telephone down. How could his leaders be so blind? They could only see their own strength and were very impressed by it. If something went wrong they simply blamed their own people for not doing their jobs.

Werner had been involved with the Luftwaffe for a long time, and he had seen its astonishing growth in just a few years. He had flown many years in biplanes. He had helped plan their use and strategy. German industry had performed miracles in building new technology.

How did we get there with such short sighted *Idioten* for leaders, he wondered. Now they think that the war is already won.

As Werner was looking out of his window, a Luftwaffe *Schwarzemann* started one of the sinister-looking *Fw-190* fighters' engines and a cloud of black smoke rolled out of its exhaust. Through the window Werner heard its harsh barking and uneven beat.

The *Schwarzemann* scowled as he shut down the engine.

The crew chief yelled, "*Was ist los?*" (what is wrong?)

The *Schwarzemann* answered "*der Motor ist kaputt.*" (the motor is ruined)

Werner was now more depressed. The sinister-looking airplanes were useless if they couldn't run properly. Not only would they not have enough new airplanes, they were going to have difficulty keeping the old ones running. Werner knew that the *Amis* had a tremendous military potential in machines. He envisioned a huge monster growing ever larger and it was heading his direction. What he couldn't know was how large it really was!

Jim

Jim was on a train heading for Texas to start his training, part of a large national build-up that would surprise even the people who were planning it. Jim did not know any of the men on the train with him very well. He had seen some of them at the reception center but had not spoken to any of them.

He had none of the anxieties that plagued many of the men. He was looking forward to new places and adventures. But looking out the window of the train, his enthusiasm flagged. He was used to looking at a high desert landscape, but this country was fast becoming monotonous. The only consolation was that he knew that the training period would be short.

When the train pulled into the station at his destination he knew the routine. Duffle bag on your shoulder, step out on the platform, don't say anything and wait quietly for someone to tell you what to do.

Those complaining and grumbling were noted by a sullen and scar-faced corporal. They would be the first ones picked to clean the toilets and do the dirty work in the kitchen. Then everyone was put on a bus and hauled a short distance to the Army base to start their basic training.

As usual, Jim was noticed out as he stepped out of the bus. He nodded a friendly smile to the sullen corporal, who immediately snapped, "Step aside, soldier." After everyone had stepped out of the bus he told Jim to move to the front of the column. In a shrill scratchy voice he shouted "I want everyone to follow this man to the barracks over there. You are to obey him. March 'em out, soldier."

Not knowing what to say, Jim decided on, "Let's go, men."

The corporal let a faint smile cross his face before he shrieked, "The proper command is, 'forward, march.'"

Jim had been prepared to be told what to do, and he was reluctantly going to do that. But now he was in charge! The young men were all staring, waiting for him to tell them what to do.

Once they reached the barracks, Jim quietly said, "Pick a bunk and put your duffle bag on it." That was easy enough. Jim threw his duffle bag on the closest bunk and the shouting started.

"That's mine," an angry recruit shouted.

Another one yelled, "Get your filthy hands off my duffle bag and your ugly face out of here."

Blows had already been thrown by the time Jim grabbed one of the recruits and threw him out of the way like a sack of grain. The rest of the recruits calmly sat down on their bunks.

The one who had started the fight immediately challenged Jim. "You're a recruit like me, and can't tell me what to do."

Jim softly asked with a slight smile, "Do you want me to show you how much authority I have? I'll throw your weak little ass out the door anytime I want to. Now shut up, sit down and wait like a good little boy."

As Jim started his training to become an aircraft mechanic, the first B-17s left the shores of North America, flew across the Atlantic and landed in England. It was only fifteen years after Lindbergh had made the first solo flight across the Atlantic. Now waves of airplanes would be flying to England to start bombing Europe.

Werner

Werner was aware of the coming crisis but knew it would be useless to report it to his superior officers. He had to work to keep enough fighters going to Russia. The Germans had only a token force there, but they had been shooting down Russian airplanes by thousands.

The exhausted Luftwaffe somehow managed to keep their worn out airplanes flying despite operating under primitive conditions.

Joachim, young German Leutnant

Joachim was one of the younger Luftwaffe pilots but he had received his training during the early stages of the war and started flying combat missions in Russia.

The Luftwaffe in Russia had been left to develop with little interference from Berlin. Staff officers did not like to subject themselves to the dangers and hardship in Russia.

The experienced pilots soon realized that they would be fighting the Russians on their own and they were going to need to train and protect the younger pilots that were sent to them. The Luftwaffe was vastly outnumbered by the Russian Air Force.

The experienced pilots became quite eager to train their students. There was plenty of combat almost every day so the inexperienced could learn very quickly. Joachim had already shot down more airplanes than the top German ace in World War One.

Since Berlin did not pay much attention to the pilots in Russia they made their own rules. The importance of rank was dropped and they decided that the pilots with the most victories would lead their combat formations.

That meant that at times sergeants led a formation with colonels following them. Joachim flew several missions a day. He had only to fly a few minutes away from his airfield before he was in the middle of Russian aircraft. The short range of the *Me-109* was no problem here. He would finish the war with almost one hundred and eighty planes shot down. His score was barely noticed among the other high-scoring Luftwaffe pilots on the Russian front.

Jim

Jim was learning about life in the military, but most of the training was about maintaining aircraft. The basic classes were easy for Jim. He had always wished that he could have finished high school, but an eighth-grade education worked well enough for him. Watching some of his classmates with a high school education struggle with the material gave Jim hope that he wasn't as uneducated as he had thought.

Werner

As some of Jim's classmates were yawning and trying to stay awake, their enemies were honing their fighting skills. The Russian front was a cruel and brutal place, but if the living was tough, shooting down Russian airplanes was fairly easy.

The *Me-109* and *Fw-190* out-performed the Russian fighters and the Luftwaffe pilots were better-trained and motivated. It led Hitler and Goering to think that they did not need to improve their airplanes or expand their pilot training program.

Libya was different. The enemy was once again the Royal Air Force. Their pilots and training were equal to the Luftwaffe's and their equipment just as good. It appeared to Werner that the Germans were going to be in trouble in the future.

One man destroyed Werner's hope of bringing reality to his commander's thinking. In Libya, Eric, a twenty-two-year-old pilot flying an *Me-109* was shooting England's best out of the sky with ease. His deflection shooting was so accurate that he only used on average fifteen rounds of ammunition to shoot down an English fighter.

That silenced anyone who said that the *Me-109* didn't have enough firepower. The feats of this one pilot only strengthened Hitler's belief in the superiority of the German people over their enemies, leading him further into his fantasy world.

When Eric shot down fifteen airplanes in one day, Hitler and Goering were sure that they couldn't lose. Some of the pilots that flew with this ace claimed that he practiced by shooting at the shadow of his comrades' airplanes as they flew low over the desert.

No one ever became as good a deflection shot as Eric. Then, the pilot who had shot down more English fighters than anyone in the Luftwaffe died suddenly while trying to bail out of his flaming *Me-109*.

Jim

As Eric's *Me-109* spun in and crashed into a sand dune in Libya, Jim was receiving his orders to train at the Boeing factory school in Seattle, Washington. So he returned over the same track he had traveled only a few months before.

He had graduated at the top of his class and was now confident that he could learn all there was to know about the bomber that Boeing was building. He also hoped that he wouldn't be put in charge of a bunch of green recruits again.

Jim enjoyed the train ride back to Seattle. He was able to get some extra rest and enjoy the fall scenery as the train rolled slowly into Oregon. He passed by towns where he had lived and worked. He noticed ranches where he had worked. But there was no time to stop and visit. Jim was going to war and he could not imagine how much he would learn in such a short time and how quickly he would be in another country.

Jim's next assignment was at the Boeing factory. The classes were taught by civilians. Jim was fascinated by all the things that he was learning. Men who had actually designed, built and flown the four-engine bomber were teaching him. He had worried that his lack of education might be a hindrance to understanding such complicated topics, but he discovered that they were easy and all he had to do was absorb the information.

When he looked around at his classmates he was always surprised when he caught them yawning and looking bored. He confronted some of them after class, "Don't you realize that this knowledge might save your life in combat?"

The younger ones would respectfully nod and say, "Yeah, you're probably right," before looking for the next card game. What Jim did not know was that the men who were less reliable were not going to be flying as a flight engineers. Instead they would have a much safer job working as ground crew.

Werner

In Russia, The German Sixth Army was surrounded. Hitler would not allow them to retreat so they were doomed. Joachim and his fellow Luftwaffe pilots were shooting down hundreds of Russian aircraft, but could not control the sky over Stalingrad. The remaining German soldiers were soon prisoners, marched into a captivity from which very few would return.

Werner was furious that his pilots were dying and suffering because of incompetent leadership. He could not say them out loud, but his mind often formed words like *Dummkopf* and *Idioten*. How could his country be led into a war by such stupid people? How was it possible that they could sacrifice their own people and not care? He hated Hitler and Goering but knew he would probably die fighting for Germany.

In Libya, the German army was pushed back towards Tripoli. The loss of Eric, their top-scoring pilot, had ended their control of the skies over Libya.

Werner was desperate to find enough fighter aircraft to fly even a few missions. He knew by now after watching Hitler sacrifice his people that he needed to get his Luftwaffe personnel out of Libya before *der Dicke* relayed Hitler's order that no one would be allowed to leave. Werner slowly removed his maintenance personnel and other important equipment from Libya. Pilots without airplanes were also flown out.

Eugen, German aircraft mechanic

Eugen had been a mechanic for the famous World War I ace, Udet. Eugen had worked on Werner's *Me-109* during the Battle of Britain. He had flown as a gunner on the *Ju-88* during the invasion of Greece and had machine-gunned English soldiers. Flying over the same area two days later he saw their bodies still lying on the road.

Next, he was in the Libyan desert, assembling *Me-109s*. The Nazi regime had enslaved thousands of people and put them to work building airplanes. Most of the workers were unskilled to begin with and they hated the Germans so their work was careless at best.

Trying to assemble these poorly built airplanes was a challenge. Now Eugen had to work in the desert heat. Most of the time the wing fitting did not match the fitting on the fuselage. Eugen used long steel bars to pry the spar fittings into place.

The pilots complained that the airplanes could not be properly trimmed in flight, but there was nothing Eugen could do about it when he had to work in such terrible conditions. The airplanes were usually destroyed in a few weeks anyway.

He was very happy when he received his orders to fly back to Germany. He was afraid that something would happen before he got out of the godforsaken desert.

He watched as an old *Ju-52* approached the landing strip. As it touched down a trail of red sand streamed briefly behind it. Its three radial engines panted a soothing familiar sound that made Eugen chuckle.

They were the same engines that he had worked on daily in the two Curtis fighters that Udet had brought back from America. The German company BMW made copies of those engines and manufactured them in metric dimensions. When the engines had shut down Eugen could not resist walking over to examine then.

He wanted to explain to the young pilots that he had worked on the original engines. Then he realized that he would be giving away his age if he did. They were probably not interested anyway.

Eugen took a seat in the old *Ju-52* and was shocked at how slow and loud she was. As they flew slowly over the blue Mediterranean Eugen couldn't help but reminisce about the time he had worked with Udet. When Hitler had begun to build the Luftwaffe, Udet had been chosen to buy airplanes from the Americans. He had bought the Curtis fighters as a civilian, so he had to pretend they were for civilian use.

He had hired Eugen to maintain them and they had toured Germany, putting on air shows. Eugen smiled as he remembered drinking cherry brandy while Udet drew scenes of air battles in World War One on the cloth napkins and sold them to the customers to pay for his and Eugen's drinks.

Eugen could see that they were approaching Sicily. He watched the smoke spiraling from Mount Etna and remembered how Udet had gone on to be director of aircraft manufacturing for all of Germany while Eugen had stayed a mechanic.

Well, Eugen was still alive and Udet had taken his own life when he could not continue to serve the Nazi cause. Mournfully, Eugen remembered that this old airplane had been built under Udet's direction. He felt like this old airplane flew: tired and sore At least he had survived this long and would continue working on airplanes the rest of his life.

Jim

As Eugen's *Ju-52* slowly settled down on the runway in Sicily, Jim was busy studying Wright aircraft engines. He not only surprised his instructors with his ability to absorb the material so quickly, he surprised himself. He had always doubted his learning ability because he had not finished high school.

His employers had seen how quickly he could learn new things, but they wanted to keep him working for them so they did not let Jim know how good he was. The course at Boeing was intense and a large amount of information was taught in a short time.

It was not long before Jim was on was on another train traveling south to Nevada for gunnery training. Jim was an excellent shot and needed very little training. The instructor used him to help others with their shooting skills. Those in charge noticed Jim's ability to lead, and it wasn't long before he was a sergeant. That would guarantee him a place as a crew member on a bomber.

Werner

Werner wished at times that he could follow Udet's example and commit suicide. Udet had been picked by Goering to take on an impossible job. Then Goering had not given him what he needed to accomplish it.

When Udet did not have enough fighters to intercept all the enemy formations, Goering and Hitler began shouting and threatening him. Udet had realized his mistake in supporting the Nazi cause. He could see no way out, except to take his own life.

Now Werner understood what Udet had gone through. In Russia the German army was in retreat. Werner's fighter command was down to less than six hundred airplanes at times. The Luftwaffe in Libya could only put up a few fighters at a time. The British and *Amis* were starting to put pressure on the Germans in Europe.

Goering had made promises to Hitler that were impossible to accomplish. Werner had tried desperately to get more fighters built and more pilots trained. Nothing had been done, but his superiors still blamed him for the bombings of Germany.

Had Werner known how quickly men like Jim were being trained and how many thousands of airplanes were coming off the assembly lines, he might have shot himself then. His days were filled with giving orders and signing documents.

He had three brothers and they were all fighter pilots. Werner was aware that when he ordered certain units into action that at least one of them would be fighting.

His head was spinning with so much action all over northern Europe. The *Amis* had started daylight bombing raids and the English were sending fighters over the continent to challenge the German fighters in the air.

The war of attrition was starting. Some units had already landed and were refueling and rearming. Werner was trying to decide if he needed to deploy them again. Different staff officers had been handing him reports all morning. One officer was standing quietly behind him.

When Werner had a break in the action he said, "*Bitte.*"

The officer reluctantly spoke. "*Ihr Bruder Paul wurde abgeschossen. Er ist tod.*" (Your brother Paul was shot down. He is dead.") Werner had been expecting all kinds of disasters to happen in his life. Somehow he thought that his family members would be exempt from death, though men were dying all around them.

As young men they had still played with trains whenever they had a chance. They had approached aerial combat as a game, and they always won. Now Werner realized that he was personally going to pay for Hitler and Goering's stupidity.

Not only was the German nation going to be defeated, but his family and everyone he knew was going to pay a price. Werner was directing hundreds of men that were fighting for their lives while all of his thoughts wanted to turn to his family.

He could not grasp how his parents would receive the news. Right now his other brothers were also in danger and he had to direct the fighter war for the rest of the day. His pride would make him carry on despite the enormity of his problems. *Es war unmenschlich*! (inhuman)

Jim

Jim had no time to rest. Hitler and Goering might think that the numbers of airplanes being produced in America was Roosevelt propaganda, but the numbers were true. Not only were the machines there but the crews to fly them were also in training.

Jim finished his gunnery training and was immediately given his orders to report to first phase training at Blythe, California. With orders in one hand and a train ticket in the other, Jim was soon sitting on a train pulling out of the station in Las Vegas, building up speed and heading for California.

As Jim settled back in his seat, one of his companions asked, "I wonder what the climate is like in Blythe?"

No one answered for a while.

Finally in a tired voice Jim said, "It won't matter much we since won't be there long enough to get used to it."

Everyone grunted in the affirmative, curled up on the seats and caught up on some much-needed sleep.

Jim knew how the military system operated, and a bus was waiting for his group with the engine running. Jim's group did not need any verbal orders and none were given.

The bus driver never left his seat and the door was open. The passengers quietly found an open seat and collapsed onto it. No one asked where they were going or why. Most went back to sleep, as if they were still on the train.

When they arrived in front of some newly built barracks, the bus stopped with squealing brakes in a cloud of dust, jolting the sleeping soldiers awake. One or two grumbled under their breaths but all stood up and quietly stepped out of the bus.

An orderly opened a door and everyone walked in, found a cot, and went back to sleep, hoping it would be for the rest of the night. These snoring men would be in the next wave of bombers challenging Hitler's highly trained and well-equipped Luftwaffe. Most of them had never flown in an airplane and had just learned how to fire a machine gun, yet they would be the eventual victors in the sky over Europe.

Emil

Emil was now flying his weary *Me-110* north over the Mediterranean Sea, since the British Eighth Army was quickly pushing the German Wehrmacht out of the Cyrenaica. He had received orders to return to Germany—*mach schnell*! (hurry up)!

He always traveled light and kept his airplane refueled and ready for take-off. He told his crew what was happening and they didn't need any coaxing or prodding to get into the airplane. They couldn't wait to get away from the *verdammte Wüste*! (damned desert)

Emil started the engines and a crewman looking at one of the motors cried out, "There is a cloud of black smoke coming out of the left motor!" Emil would have to break his number one rule about not taking unnecessary risks. Flying over a large body of water with a worn out engine was one of them

He did not know exactly where the English Army was located, but it was only seconds before Emil was pushing the throttles to full power and a cloud of red dust billowed out behind his airplane, mixed with a trace of oil. He had not climbed more than a few meters before he could see the clouds of dust stirred up by the Tommy tanks. They were only a few kilometers away from the airstrip he had just left behind.

It was the right decision and the only option, but now he was where he had never wanted to be. It would depend on luck and the word luck had never been in Emil's vocabulary. He had seen too many men deserted by it.

Now he was committed, thinking of how to get a longer life out of a dying engine. This airplane's engines did not have the extra air filter installed in many of the airplanes flying in the desert. The fine Libyan red sand had slowly worn away the engine's piston rings and cylinder walls. The left engine would eventually blow its lubricating oil out into the slipstream.

Emil wanted to slow down the speed at which the engine was turning. The problem was that he then had to use a higher manifold pressure, blowing even more oil away. He decided to use the normal power setting and hope for the best. He could not pass up the thought that if it had not been for Hitler's insanity, he would not be in this dangerous situation.

The oil pressure slowly dropped and the cylinder head temperature rose. The left engine would often shudder, causing the anxious crew members to look at their pilot for reassurance.

Emil looked as unperturbed as he could. He knew he could fly on the right engine for a while, but it had the same history as the left engine and did not need more stress. The left engine was shuddering more often now. Emil was ready to feather the engine immediately before it lost oil pressure.

He had set his course for Sicily after takeoff from Libya. He was worried that English fighters might intercept him, but that was not his biggest concern. Now the left engine was shaking so badly he worried that it might shake itself loose from it mounts.

Reluctantly he reached for the propeller control, feathered the engine and shut it down all in one motion. He added power to right engine to keep up his airspeed.

He did all of this so quickly that the crew members did not have time to be afraid. They had flown with this *alten Adler* (old eagle) through several harrowing months in the *Wüste*, avoiding British fighters. They felt confident that he would get them through this experience too.

Emil was not that sure, but he was scanning the horizon for land. He did not spot land right away but saw smoke on the horizon. One of the crew members exclaimed, "*Vieso raucht es vor uns?*" (why is it smoking up there?)

Emil quietly answered, "Those are the Sicilians sending us a smoke signal. They are giving us permission to land."

He waited a moment and said, "If you ever wanted to worship a volcano, make it Mt Etna. There is an airfield at Catania - we might just make it."

The right engine was starting its death throes, shuddering and smoking. Emil made a straight approach heading west. Wrecked aircraft lined both sides of the runway. Emil paid no attention to them and like the expert that he was, made a perfect landing, taxied to the headquarters, and shut down the right engine which clanked to a stop, never to run again. None of the personnel at the airport even looked their direction; aircraft in that condition landed here all the time.

Emil was soon sent back to Germany. Now that the Wehrmacht was retreating on most fronts, aerial pictures weren't needed as much. Staff officers looking for more fighter pilots saw Emil's records and noted that he had trained as a fighter pilot and he was soon assigned to a fighter unit.

He was still a *Feldwebel* with almost five years of combat. Most of the officers were younger and less experienced than Emil. They eyed him with suspicion, since they didn't care for someone with less rank and more experience watching them. Since he was older and had a quiet temperament he didn't fit the picture of the wild partying fighter pilot. His commanding officer realized that someone with lower rank leading a *Staffel* might cause problems with some of the younger officers.

Kurt

Kurt was getting his share of the fighting now that the *Amis* were starting their bombing raids. The day fighters had not seen much action when the English bombed at night. But now the *Amis* thought that they could bomb in the day time.

When the Germans had bombed England in the daytime, they'd learned the hard way that they could not afford the loss of so many bombers. The English had also learned that they could not afford the causalities of daylight bombing. The *Amis* could. They made some small raids and were not discouraged by the loss of a few planes.

Kurt was fast learning to score in combat and his victories were slowly rising. He had painted a large number thirteen on his airplane. He wanted everyone to remember him—both friend and foe. He had already forced several airplanes to surrender and land at a German airfield. He had shot an American fighter down over England. That *Ami* would see that number thirteen again over Europe.

Hans

Hans was becoming an excellent fighter pilot. He was a good shot in the air and he knew how to maneuver to get into the right firing position. He had never learned how to control the *Me-109* on landing and had bent several airplanes. All those technical things did not interest him.

He didn't care that the *Schwarzemänner* didn't like him. His job was to kill the enemy and theirs was to take care of his machine. It never occurred to him that a disgruntled mechanic might sabotage his airplane. He became more sullen and bitter the longer he flew. He drank more and more, but mostly alone. Many of his fellow pilots were doing the same. The ground personnel hated him and his superior officers were careful in how they approached him.

Jim

Jim awoke to a different world the next morning. He was no longer a recruit learning the simple rules of the military; he was a part of an elite group who had mastered all the courses that had washed out many of the candidates who had started.

Now he was training to be a flight engineer on a four-engine bomber. It was just eight months since he had left the ranch for the Army. Now what he had learned in school was going to be applied to real airplanes.

The flight engineer had many tasks. He did all the pre-flight inspections, monitored the refueling of the airplane and supervised the crew chief. On take-off and landing he stood behind the pilots, checking all the engine instruments. When needed, he moved fuel from one tank to another.

Besides that, he was the top turret gunner. Jim had already graduated from gunnery school, and finished the factory school on B-17s. Now that things were getting serious, even the younger gunners were doing less clowning around and learning to do their job right. They were part of a team and their job was important for everyone's survival.

The pilots, navigators and bombardiers were all officers. Jim's job as senior sergeant was to make sure everyone on the crew did what they were supposed to. Even the officers were checked by the flight engineer to make sure all their equipment was properly cared for.

It was definitely exciting when Jim's class was introduced to the B-17. To men who had just recently left their farms and ranches, the bomber looked huge. Four complicated engines to maintain and operate was overwhelming to some who had never flown before.

The instructors were showing them all the cockpit instruments and explaining their use. Jim could only chuckle when he thought of what was expected of him. Fortunately he was issued manuals that he could study afterwards. There was not going to be much spare time. The training went on fourteen hours a day. They were going to be needed in England soon.

In Europe the Eighth Air Force made its first bombing raid on Wilhelmshafen. It was the first American bombing raid into Germany. Jim was not aware of the raid, but it was only a few months before he would be flying in the same type of aircraft over the same terrain, and he wasn't even finished with his training. He couldn't imagine in how short a time he would be in combat.

Werner

Werner had more information about the war than Jim did, but it did not give him any comfort. Nazi propaganda was claiming glorious victory over the inexperienced *Amis*. Goering gloated about what the Luftwaffe would do to them if they tried to continue their bombing. Since he insisted on rejecting any information coming from the German intelligence agency, he was content with believing what he formed in his own sick mind.

Werner believed the information that he was receiving, though he wished it weren't true. The American training system was pouring thousands of men into hastily constructed camps. They started their training instantly, as men like Jim left one camp for the next, someone would take their place the next day.

He could draw a picture in his mind of a long monster crawling slowly across America swallowing people and resources growing larger and larger with each day. This monster was headed towards Germany. Werner visualized the Luftwaffe cutting off the head sometimes, but still the monster would keep growing.

The pilots attacking the *Ami* formations had no doubts about the impossibility of their task. The Americans were going to get better and better with each day as their crews gained experience. Right now the highly experienced Luftwaffe pilots had an advantage. As younger and less experienced men replaced them there would be problems.

Right now most of the Luftwaffe pilots felt optimistic about their chances against the *Amis'* bombers. They were receiving a new fighter and were impressed with its performance. The *Fw-190* was an easier airplane to fly than the *Me-109*. Its wider landing gear make it easier to land. In combat against the English fighters it was faster.

When the pilots first saw the new airplane they were disappointed to see that it had two fuel tanks underneath the pilot's seat. The *Me-109* was built the same way. The English fighter pilots had always commented that they felt sorry for the Jerry pilots because they were sitting directly over their fuels tanks which burned if hit by tracer bullets.

73

The engineers had discovered that the canopy on the *Fw-190* could not be easily released if the pilot needed to bail out. They had devised a method using the shell from a 20mm cannon placed on each side of the canopy. Push a button and the explosive charge would blow the canopy off. Now all the pilot had to do was jump out of his seat and hope that he didn't get hit by the tail plane.

Kurt

Maybe that was why Kurt would be wounded fourteen times in the war. He had to worry about getting shot down by the enemy and if he was shot down he could be injured by his own aircraft hitting him. Right now he was trying to find a way to knock the *vier Mots* (four motors) out of the air.

Kurt began by watching the German fighters attacking the bombers. When they had first begun to attack the B-17s, they attacked from the rear. That left the fighters vulnerable to the fire from the tail gunner in the bomber. The tail gunner had two fifty caliber machine guns that could reach the German fighter before his own guns were in range. One pilot said it was like taking a shower in hot lead.

The B-17s had guns covering every conceivable position. The front was covered by a hydraulic turret that was sure to shoot down any fighter it got in its sights. Kurt decided to experiment by attacking one bomber head on but just a few degrees lower than the enemy plane. He discovered that the gunner could not see that area because the nose of the bomber obscured his vision.

So now all the German pilots had to do was attack head on and a little low. It took nerves of steel, lightning quick reflexes and a lot of skill. The incentive to do it right was the fact that if you didn't, you would probably be shot down. Kurt kept experimenting, working with another pilot to form new methods of attacking the B-17's defenses. Then they began training other pilots in the technique.

Jim

Jim's training moved at an exhausting pace. He was learning so many details he doubted he could remember all of them. The squabbling that had been so common among the soldiers in all the other phases was over. Everyone knew that they would soon be fighting for their lives and at night they were exhausted, going right to sleep.

In the next phase they were formed into crews. The pilots who received Jim as a flight engineer felt lucky. They liked his confident attitude and knowledge of the B-17. They gave him the responsibility of leading the crew.

The training continued to be intense and there was little time to relax. At times they left some of the gunners on the ground because they were not needed.

As flight engineer, Jim was on every flight and involved in maintenance on the airplanes. Now they were talking to men who had actually flown in combat. It was not very encouraging. The Luftwaffe pilots flew excellent fighters and the pilots were crazy, flying through a hail of bullets to attack the bombers. Jim hoped he could shoot as well as any German pilot.

Werner

I f Werner could have seen how fast Jim and his crew were advancing in their training and that they were training in new aircraft just a few weeks off the assembly line he would have been even more discouraged. It was difficult to fight for a lost cause and even more horrible to think about sending other men to die for that lost cause.

He would have quit but for some close friends who pleaded with him to stay. They argued that if he left, a less competent political appointee would be put in charge and the fighter command would lose even more pilots.

The remnant of experienced pilots were exhausted. They were well trained, and they often joked they could shoot down enemy planes in their sleep. They needed to as they were continually in the air and always fighting.

American bomber crew

If someone had written music to the time that Jim was living in, it would have been a drum roll constantly picking up speed. The ground officers that had often given men petty orders to do useless jobs faded into the background. These flight crews were soon going to be in a desperate situation.

Those who had felt superior to these lower-ranking people realized that they were doing something only the very brave could do. The drum roll slowly picked up speed as Jim realized it would not be long before he would be fighting for his life. It gave him some consolation when he thought about his former boss and their last conversation.

Jim had to grin when he thought about his boss spending long hours in the hot sun trying to do Jim's work. All over America people were doing work that they had never thought they would need to do, and they were glad to do it as long as they did not have to sacrifice their lives and suffer like those in the service of their county.

Even the young gunners realized that life was becoming more serious. They were leaving the teenage life behind and became more serious and a little despondent. It made Jim's life much easier. He had never enjoyed baby-sitting his crew.

The officers were busy training and learning as much as they could about their work as possible. Men who a short time ago had never been in an airplane, were flying the modern bombers. The veteran test pilots who had just started to understand these aircraft had to put them in the hands of twenty-year-olds just out of high school.

Likewise, the men learning aerial navigation, had never been in the air before entering training. The bomb sight that the young bombardiers were training to use had just been invented and was considered top secret.

The radio operators were also trained as gunners. Most of the gunners were younger, but their job was to protect the airplane and other crew members from the attacking Luftwaffe fighters. Firing the fifty caliber machine guns in training had been great fun. Firing from a moving airplane was completely different.

If you enjoyed flying it wasn't that bad. For those who didn't like to fly, it was frightening. It was bad enough when the instructors were explaining how to wear the parachute, but when they showed how to slip and steer it after jumping from an airplane some just closed their eyes and promised themselves never to jump, no matter the consequences.

The men being taught how to wear and use the parachute were never given a chance to actually jump from an airplane. If they had been given an opportunity, many probably would have refused. The Air Corp would have had to find someone else to take their place and the pace of the training would have slowed.

Jim's work training the crew to get along with each other got easier, but now he had other problems. He could threaten and cuss, but certain ones would still forget how important it was to watch the flow of oxygen when they were flying at high altitude, and some also forgot important pieces of equipment. No matter how angry Jim got, he had to watch all the crew members to make sure they were performing their duties. Then he had to make sure that the bomber was maintained as it should be.

On takeoff he stood behind the pilots, watching every move they made. As the airplane gained speed he would call out the airspeed until they had retracted the landing gear and he watched to make sure that the flaps were securely up. Though he complained and cussed, he was in his element, doing something that he had never dreamed of but aware that he was working with the very best men his country could produce.

Now the time had arrived to graduate. The diploma would be a trip to England and they would do all the flying themselves. They were issued a new B-17. They had little time to admire the plane before they prepared for a test flight.

A loudmouth captain shoved stack of papers at the pilot and told him to sign immediately. Looking briefly at the documents, the pilot realized that he was signing papers that said he had inspected the bomber and that it was one hundred percent airworthy and did not need any further maintenance. When questioned, the captain curtly told them to ignore all the little problems. Those details could be taken care of in England.

The captain shouted, "If I say the airplane is airworthy then you are ordered to take my word for it."

The pilot of Jim's airplane, a lieutenant who was older than the captain, stared incredulously at him for a moment, then handed back the papers, unsigned. Without a word, he nodded to his crew to enter the airplane.

The insulted captain screamed at them as the first engine belched out smoke and started to rumble, "That's an order, and I could court martial you if you disobey."

Now all four engines were running, the pilot added power to taxi and as the big bomber turned toward the runway, the captain's best hat flew off his head and he had to quickly run to catch it.

During the test flight Jim was busy writing down all the defects he could find, and there were many. The Air Corp was pushing to get the airplanes to England as quickly as possible. The officers in the chain of command were flying a very secure desk. They wanted to look good to their superiors so they pushed those who were flying.

The factory owners were getting rich fast, but you could never make too much money. The labor shortage allowed them to hire anyone they could find. They were happily building complicated machinery with unskilled labor. They gave orders to their supervisors to get the airplanes built as fast as possible. Don't worry about mistakes. These bombers were only going to be shot down anyway.

Jim's new airplane was going to need some work before it could be flown to England. The stony face of Jim's pilot kept the staff officers away and Jim managed to bribe and coerce supply men and any mechanic that wasn't busy at the moment. They were able to bring the new bomber up to a safe condition. The staff officers squirmed as they watched what was going on but were forced to wait until the crews approved the airplanes for flight.

When Jim's B-17 taxied out to begin its long flight to England, some of the ground officers felt guilty as they watched these men, many of whom would never return to their homes. But that feeling didn't last long and mostly they were happy that someone else was taking their place.

With a roar, Jim's bomber climbed quickly away from the airfield. They were still in sight when the next new bomber arrived from the factory. The captain sighed and hoped he would have better luck intimidating the next crew.

While Jim and the pilots were busy watching the gauges on the new engines, the other crew members were watching the landscape of Nebraska slide under the wings of the airplane. Everything was green and the crops looked great. Jim gave a quick glance at the endless fields of corn and thought, "at least I won't need to harvest those crops."

Now as Jim's bomber droned across the land, the crew saw how large their country was. Watching the landscape change from the air, they surveyed the bread basket of the Midwest, large rivers, farms, and the larger towns. Roads connected all of them. Smoke rose in the air from thousands of chimneys.

From their altitude, Jim's crew could not see the millions of people working to produce weapons of war. The parts in their bomber came from many different places in America.

Now, with bellowing engines, it sounded like the roaring monster Werner had visualized, coming from the West to attack his country and its people. Hitler and Goering kept ignoring the threat; they had closed their minds and refused to acknowledge that a monster war machine much larger than theirs was headed their way.

The navigator in Jim's bomber proudly announced their position over the intercom as they steadily flew eastward. He felt a great sense of accomplishment when he could state with authority, "Approaching on the left side of the airplane you can see Lake Erie."

The young navigator sighed with relief that he had managed to bring the bomber this far without getting lost. Now leaving the city of Cleveland behind to the left side, he could see Lake Ontario approaching on the same side. In the distance the city of Rochester greeted him, visible on the lake's south shore.

He was gaining confidence as he spotted the Adirondack Mountains rising in the distance. The young man convinced himself that aerial navigation might not be as difficult as many had said it might be.

The crew of Jim's bomber watched the landscape of New England move slowly under the wing of the bomber. Spring had every tree leaf and flower blooming in full color. They could only wonder what might await them in England.

Happily, the navigator gave the pilots the last heading for Bangor, Maine, and gave a sigh of relief when he heard the pilots talking to the tower operators there.

Jim was now standing behind the pilots, watching as they slowly retarded the power to the engines. As they slowed down, the landing gear began to moan and the wheels slid out of their comfortable home in the wheel well. Everyone breathed out with relief when the green lights came on, showing that the landing gear was down and locked.

The bomber was now lined up with the runway and the co-pilot lowered the wing flaps a few degrees. Slowly, the pilot raised the nose a little and the bomber settled onto the runway, the tires screeching in protest.

Tired crew members dropped out of the escape hatches and looked at their surroundings. Some asked where they would sleep but most wondered where they would eat. A truck drove up and stopped in front of them.

"Get in," ordered an unkempt enlisted man.

The crews were immediately dropped in front of a mess hall and told to go and get something to eat. They had barely finished their meal before another hungry crew was ready to take their place. Bombers were continuously landing and ground crews were desperately trying to find places to park them.

Werner

Werner was reading the intelligence reports and knew that hundreds of airplanes were headed his way, intent on destroying Hitler and the Nazi system. Werner despised the Nazis but he could not separate Germany from its cruel government, so he would continue to fight for a cause he hated and was sure it could not win.

Despite the odds, Luftwaffe fighter pilots were shooting down thousands of Soviet airplanes. Still, the Wehrmacht was losing ground to the Russian Army. It was difficult for any rational person to ignore the fact that Germany could not win the conflict. Neither Hitler nor Goering were rational people.

Germany had already flown the first jet fighter. It would have been a great weapon in the hands of the Luftwaffe fighter pilots. Werner could not believe his ears when he heard Hitler proclaim that they were going to use it as a bomber!

Jim

Bangor, Maine was a staging base for bombers flying to England. There was a lack of mechanics and parts for the gathering airplanes. Jim had a long list of maintenance items he wanted to repair before they flew over water and the wilderness of Newfoundland. He did not know exactly what their route would be but wanted a perfectly running airplane before he left.

He started looking for someone to help find parts for his Bomber. The permanent staff was swamped with work and no one would stop long enough to talk to him. The pilot of his airplane advised him to stop looking. Maybe they could find what they needed at the Gander, Newfoundland base.

The orders came much too soon for the B-17 crew. *Take off tomorrow morning; if all four engines are running you will go.* The simple briefing claimed it was nothing more than a training flight. The last part of the briefing was a message from a seemingly uncertain meteorologist who did not care to look the crews in the face. He couldn't imagine flying over the Atlantic Ocean in one of those airplanes.

The navigators were given the details of the flight and everyone was driven to their airplanes.

The co-pilot nervously kept asking Jim, , "Have you checked the fuel? Are all the fuel caps tightened?"

Jim finally told him to shut up and leave him alone. When everyone was settled in, the pilots started the engines and moved to their place behind another bomber. The large bombers started the takeoff roll with a roar.

Jim was always excited during takeoff and steadily called out their airspeed to the pilots. Landing gear up. retract flaps, retard power to climb revolutions. Everyone sighed with relief as they settled into a loose formation with the other bombers.

The navigator was enjoying his trade. He spotted Saint John, Canada on the shore of the Bay of Fundy. Cape Chignecto obligingly appeared at the proper time and all he had to do was follow Nova Scotia north-east to Grace Bay.

As they passed over Sydney, Nova Scotia, the pilot spoke over the intercom to the crew, "Take a good look—this might be the last time you see North America." It certainly would be for him!

It was a long time before anyone spoke again. Now they were over the water, the beautiful check points were gone, with only miles of empty ocean staring back at them. The navigator despairingly realized that now his job was going to be more difficult. At least he was not alone, and all the pilot had to do was follow the other bombers to Gander. Hopefully the lead navigator knew what he was doing.

In less than an hour, a long thin line appeared on the eastern horizon. To men who had lived their lives on land, they felt like the early explorers finding a new continent. There were little towns scattered along the coast of Newfoundland. But they passed swiftly and the navigator didn't have enough time to identify them.

Silently, the crew watched a beautiful but strange landscape slide beneath their wings. Mountains and lakes were in abundance. Like tourists, they thought they would like to visit this place some other time. They all realized they would need to survive a brutal war before that happened.

Now the same routine started with the co-pilot reading from the checklist in preparation for landing. Out of a gray Newfoundland sky the B-17s glided toward Gander Field. The recently constructed airfield was not very exciting to the tired crews. At least they hoped they would be fed and find a place to sack out.

It was not long before the formation of B-17's roared and staggered into the gray skies, once more, now headed east. Their bombers were heavy with more than a full load of fuel, which they would need it if wanted to get to Scotland. Everyone was solemn as the heavy bombers slowly climbed to their cruising altitude.

Jim intently watched the engine instruments for any sign of problems. He didn't see any. The sober faces of his crew were frightening, and he realized that the next stop would bring them into the war.

The navigator had nothing to do as he had no check points. The lead airplane had a drift meter but that was all. The good news was that they had a tail wind that would save some fuel. Now everyone that did not have to fly the airplane went to sleep. The bomber formation droned its way across an empty Atlantic Ocean.

The navigator was standing in Jim's place between the pilots since he wanted to be the first to spot Ireland. Since leaving Bangor, Maine he realized that he had a lot to learn about aerial navigation. If he got lost it might cost everyone their lives.

Then out of the haze he saw a fine line on the horizon. He waited a few moments to be sure, tapped the pilot on the shoulder and announced, "I see land ahead."

The pilot had to raise his body to see better, then exclaimed' "I hope that is Ireland, because if it's not, we're lost."

The navigator had spent the last few hours studying his map and proudly said, "I see the Main Head." The hook-like point indicates the northern-most part of Ireland.

Now all the crew was awake. With the sighting of land, they were back in a world they understood. The navigator now was in his element, announcing one checkpoint after another as the right wing of the B-17 pointed towards the northern part of Ireland. Like a tour guide, he pointed out to everyone that they were now flying the North Channel approaching Sana Island. They would shortly be landing in Prestwick, Scotland.

The crew was impressed with their navigator's ability to find his way across the ocean. The pilot was also pleased that the young man was actually learning to navigate. The co-pilot reached for the landing checklist and wearily began reading off each item.

On the ground in Scotland it did not take the Air Corp long to place the crew on a train, and once again Jim was looking out the window at an unfamiliar landscape, wondering what was going to happen next.

Tired as he was, the navigator studied the west coast of Scotland. There were scores of checkpoints on the rugged coast and he thought it might be helpful to remember them. As the train moved further south into England, the view became less exciting and the navigator joined the rest of the crew and went to sleep

Jim's crew stepped off of the train and were driven to their new home. It was one of the better air bases in England. They had a permanent building to live in and even had some heat. It was definitely better than the Quonset huts used by the other crews.

The corporal showing them their billets proudly said that they were very lucky to be stationed so close to London. Of course he was not one who was going to be flying bombers over Europe. No one knew at that time that more B-17s would be lost from this airfield than any other base in England. There would not be much time for enjoying the nightlife of London. They could see the German bombs falling on the city at night.

When they walked into the mess hall for their first meal, only a few of the men already eating even looked up. The men who had already been in combat didn't want to know the new crews. It was already established that the new men would suffer the highest casualty rates. They had already lost friends and now they were looking forward to just getting in their twenty-five missions and going home.

When Jim's crew was at last assigned to a bomber, it was one which looked worse for wear. It had patches all over where it had been damaged in combat. The paint was peeling in many places and the engines were dripping oil.

The crew was shocked. They had delivered a new airplane and now they had to fly some junk. Jim's mechanical instincts were insulted, but he found the crew chief. He wanted to learn more about the condition of the bomber they were going to fly.

When he approached the sergeant responsible for maintaining his airplane he saw a tired, overworked man who had not seen a full night's rest in a long time. All the men around him were in the same condition. He explained to Jim that the most he could accomplish in maintenance was to take care of the most important items and ignore the rest. There were B-17s flying with tape covering some of the instruments. The crews knew that if they turned their bomber in for higher echelon maintenance they might receive another bomber in even worse condition. Because it was uncomfortable to stare at an instrument that was showing a problem with an engine they just put tape over it and ignored it.

Jim couldn't wait to start fixing up his airplane. But before he could pick up a wrench the next morning, he was informed by the pilot that they were going on a training flight and to pre-flight the airplane to fly in an hour. So much for working on it.

The pace quickened, and Jim's crew trained daily on formation flying and staying close to other airplanes in the air. This was no longer a relaxed training flight like they had done in the States. The men training them knew that their lives would depend on how well the new crews performed in formation flying. There was no room for error.

Kurt

Kurt was quick to apply his new attack methods, but he needed to learn patience and wait for the right opening before he attacked. He could not get past the feeling that he was killing someone who might have been a friend.

That feeling sometimes caused him to be shot down and even be wounded. He always tried to make the damaged enemy aircraft surrender by landing at German-controlled airfields. It had worked several times and his superior officers pretended to look the other way. They were not too worried that any other pilots would be crazy or confident enough to try to copy Kurt's actions.

Kurt had the big number thirteen painted on his fighter. He damaged an *Ami* P-47 one day in a fight over Belgium. The pilot of the P-47 recognized the thirteen painted on the nose of the German fighter; he had been shot down over England by a German fighter with the same number painted on it. When Kurt had signaled for him to surrender he had reluctantly lowered his landing gear and started a descent to the nearest airfield.

As he approached the runway he saw many German anti-aircraft guns sighting in on him. His guns were still armed and all he had to do was press the trigger and add full power to his engine. He went past the guns so fast that by the time they fired, they hit Kurt's fighter, which immediately crashed. It sent Kurt to the hospital with another serious wound.

Twenty years later the American pilot walked into Kurt's store and discovered that he was the pilot of number thirteen. The American never received credit for shooting Kurt down because they couldn't confirm that he had crashed and even if he had, German gunners had shot him down. No one knows how many American lives were saved while Kurt was recovering in the hospital, unable to attack American bombers.

Hans

Hans was no longer a young, inexperienced pilot. He had acquired the necessary confidence to shoot enemy aircraft from the sky. He maintained his distance from most of the other people around him with his sullen look and blood-shot eyes.

These were the men that Jim and his crew would soon be facing in combat. They were now watching the B-17 formations taking off on their missions and later returning hours later with many bombers missing.

Many of the returning bombers fired red flares to let the control tower know that they had wounded on board. Some planes landed with the landing gear still retracted because of damage to their airplane.

The crews still in training could only watch and wonder when their turn would come. They were told that after twenty-five missions their tour of duty would be over. Then the instructor mentioned that the average number of missions flown before being shot down was five.

Five members of the crew usually would survive though of course they would probably be prisoners of war. The Eighth Air Force would lose twenty-six thousand men killed in action over Europe.

Most of the men in Jim's crew became quieter with each day. Most of the excitement that they had felt before was gone, replaced with a determination to do their job as best they could. The pilots were concentrating on formation flying and keeping their place tight within the formation. Jim did not need to tell the younger crewmen the importance of maintaining their equipment.

Their first mission was a long one—they were leading a group of fighters to Cairo, Egypt. Their young navigator was excited to be chosen to lead the flight. The rest of the crew was mostly bored, though the pilots were happy to get more flying hours in before they went into combat. They were all relieved when they returned and landed in England.

Jim would later exclaim, "You can a see lot of the world sitting in the top turret of a B-17!"

It was not long before Jim's crew was awakened at two AM and told to get ready for a mission. Too stunned to complain, they dressed silently and without a word walked to the mess hall for breakfast.

Some had hoped that they would have time to think about what it was like to go on a combat mission. The trip to the waiting bombers did not take long and they were busy getting their equipment together. No one had to tell them to make sure their machine guns were working properly.

Still, Jim watched every move they made and checked everything twice. The pilots had no time to be nervous. They watched and counted the number of engine rotations, turned on the ignition switch and were relieved when all four engines were running with a lusty roar. Jim quickly scanned all the engine instruments; everything was in order.

The rest of the crew had nothing to do until they were airborne, except they had more time to think and ponder what might happen. The navigator was disappointed that all the pilots had to do was follow the leader. He would only be needed if they fell out of formation.

The bombardier would only need to drop his bombs when he saw the bomber in front of him drop his. The bombers slowly waddled down the taxiway to the runway. Already the first bomber was airborne as some bombers were still on the taxiway.

Bomber after bomber staggered into the air. The pilots were busy flying and Jim continuously checked engine instruments.

The rest of the crew was trying to act nonchalant by checking their gear. Their thoughts never ranged far from the fact that they were would be in combat in a short time.

The bomber wing found its way towards Europe, and over the English Channel the co-pilot gave orders for everyone to load their guns and test fire them. As they gained altitude the next order was to go on oxygen. Jim watched and listened to make sure everyone was using his oxygen.

The flight to Kassel, Germany was longer than some missions but before they arrived, the wing commander gave the order to turn back to England. That part of Germany was covered in clouds. So their first mission was no more than a training flight.

They had gotten a break, but the next morning they were back in the air, the Germans determined to stop them from bombing the submarine pens at

Kiel, Germany. The Luftwaffe had misjudged the target of the bombers and as the result they did not send enough fighters to stop them.

Still, Jim was able to get his first shots at an enemy aircraft. He was surprised how easy it was to hit a moving airplane. He saw the *Me-109* smoking badly after his machine guns bullets had struck it in the engine.

Another crew said they had seen the pilot bail out, since he had no desire to stay with a burning airplane while sitting on top of a fuel tank.

The Germans were wary of attacking with insufficient fighters, especially after they had seen one of their comrades sprayed with bullets and shot down. Jim was given credit for shooting down the *Me-109*. Other gunners in other bombers tried to claim credit, but so many witness had seen Jim's shots hit the *Me-109* that he was given the credit.

The weather was good the next day so Jim's B-17 was airborne early the next morning. They were heading for Kassel Germany, the same target of their first aborted mission. Now Jim's crew felt like they were experienced enough to take anything the Luftwaffe could throw at them.

German Pilots

On the status board, Werner watched the progression of the bomber formation as it approached the Continent. He noticed that it was flying almost the same route that the *Amis* had flown on another raid when they tried to bomb Kassel two days before. He was sure that they would try again.

Soon the loudspeakers on the Luftwaffe fighter bases along that route were broadcasting the alarm. The radial engines on the *Fw-190s* bellowed out their uneven roar. The Mercedes engines on the *Me-109s* sounded smoother and gave out a loud roar as they climbed away from the airfield.

Kurt watched as his *Staffel* formed up behind him. He hated killing other men but combat flying was very exciting and he was happy to get enough warning to gain some altitude before attacking the enemy.

Hans was now a confident fighter pilot. He enjoyed the performance of his new *Fw-190*. He felt a rush of excitement as he climbed swiftly higher and heard the controller excitedly giving the fighter *Staffel* commander the position of the bomber formation.

Jim

Jim's crew members were continually reporting enemy fighters climbing up from airfields below. Jim had a good view of his formation and was pleased to see that most of the B-17s were holding their positions in the formation.

Jim watched a formation of eight *Fw-190s* flying parallel to the bombers. They stayed out of range of the 50-caliber machine guns on the bombers and soon pulled ahead of the bomber formation. Jim set his sight for the wing-span of one *Fw-190* and watched as the fighters started to turn towards them.

Kurt

K urt watched his flight of eight fighters swing into a straight line as they hurled themselves straight at the oncoming bombers, closing in at an unbelievable speed. Bullets from the bombers started pouring out at the fighters.

Kurt felt his plane shake as the bullets struck its armor, then he pressed his cannon's firing button. The 20 mm cannon shells walked across the wing of the B-17 and Kurt rolled his airplane just in time to miss the bomber's large rudder.

Jim

When the German fighter's wing tips touched both sides of Jim's sight he started firing. He decided at these speeds to let that Jerry run right into his gunfire. Pieces flew off the *Fw-190* and Jim kept firing until the fighter dropped away, burning.

Jim grinned and announced that he had just shot down another Jerry. Nobody was listening; bombers were dropping out of the sky and some had just blown up, parachutes scattering behind them. A few Luftwaffe fighters crashed into the ground. The bomber pilots were flying as close as they could to the next airplane in the formation.

Kurt

Kurt kept the nose of his *Fw-190* pointed straight ahead and his engine at full power while tracer bullets flew at him from all directions. He pulled up once he was out of the range of the bomber's guns.

He spotted his wingman close behind him, but the rest of his flight was scattered all over the sky. He made a wide turn, attempting to get ahead of the bomber formation. Two of his *Staffel* joined him.

He knew that with fewer fighters attacking the bombers, there would be more machine guns firing at each of his fighters, but he turned toward the bomber formation and hoped for the best.

Jim

J im watched the four German fighters start their attack. He was confident that he could shoot down at least one more fighter. Flak bursts came faster now as they approached their target. He knew that normally the German pilots did not like to attack while their anti-aircraft fire exploded among the bombers.

Jim saw that the *Fw-190s* coming at them were not turning away. This time he opened fire sooner than he was taught to do in gunnery school and watched pieces fly off the German fighter. It broke off its attack and dove out of sight.

Jim saw another B-17 burning behind him and then felt his bomber bounce upward as it dropped three tons of bombs on Kassel. The German flak kept firing, but Kurt had ordered his *Staffel* to return to their home base.

After the Amis had dropped their bombs, the German fighter pilots were not as aggressive as at the beginning of the battle. Jim had expected the Germans to attack the bomber formation but had been surprised by their ferocity. Jim realized that the Luftwaffe pilots were going to fight to the death. Turning back to England, he saw smoke from the B-17s that had been shot down on the flight to Kassel. It was very quiet on their return home and nobody felt like celebrating.

Kurt

K urt landed and shut down his engine but stayed in his cockpit, listening to the engine ticking as it cooled down. He counted the number of fighters parked on the ramp. His whole *Staffel* was there, but bullet holes pockmarked many of them and some had panels shot off. At least they had survived to fight another day. The problem was that the Ami bombers had gotten through to bomb Kassel.

Jim

Jim's bomber landed with most of its squadron intact, but there were several empty parking spots where the ground crew kept scanning the sky in the hope that their bomber might return. Jim's crew members were exhausted and stunned by the Luftwaffe's ferocious attacks. At the beginning of their tour they had hoped that as they gained experience, they would be able to survive in the air over Germany. Now they were certain that it was just a matter of time before they would be shot down. The good news was, that they would have time before the next mission.

Hans

Hans had shot down another B-17 in the fight. He landed and turned off his fighter's engine. When he approached the orderly room the adjutant remarked that his *Gruppe* was done flying for the day. He cautiously asked Hans if he had scored any victories during the fight.

Hans replied, "I shot down one just north of Kassel and I damaged another after the bombing run."

The adjutant thanked Hans and said, "I'll see if I can get that confirmed."

Hans was already walking towards the club to start drinking. He didn't want to think about flying.

Kurt

Kurt was studying the tactics the Luftwaffe was using against the bomber formations. The head-on attack worked very well if he could keep seven or eight fighters attacking together. After the first attack his fighters scattered and he could only bring three or four fighters for the second round.

The head-on attack unnerved the attackers as much as it did the attacked. Kurt knew that the more experienced pilots had a higher survival rate than the beginners. He was certain that one of the reasons that he had such difficulty reorganizing for the second attack was that some of the less experienced pilots were too rattled to go through with another one.

Jim

J im's crew had several days off from flying. Jim spent most of his time helping the mechanics work on his bomber. Everyone knew it would not be long before they would be flying again. The weather in the middle of August was the best time of year in Europe. New bombers and crew arrived daily at his airfield. More people for the Germans to shoot down.

The next mission was to bomb German-held airfields in France. Jim's crew now dreaded any combat mission. The confidence and proficiency they had acquired in their first mission had been replaced with the reality that their chances of survival were poor. They were certain the Luftwaffe pilots would not give them any quarter.

Still, when the engines on their B-17 started and belched out clouds of smoke they felt a sense of relief and excitement. Watching one bomber after another climbing into the gray English sky impressed them with the fact they were making history on a massive scale. The targets in France were not a great distance for the long-range bombers, but they would be stirring up a hornets' nest.

The German fighters would be swarming all over them, even with American escort fighters present. Even with no fighters attacking they would still be shot at by Flak. Jim did not need to tell the other crew members to check their weapons and equipment. They had received their lessons from the Luftwaffe and weren't looking forward to any more instruction.

Werner

Werner had been informed about the pending Ami bombing mission. There were some diversionary missions already in the air. They appeared to be heading for the usual targets. The radar reports indicated they were heading more to the west than usual. Now his problem would be getting enough fighters into the air to intercept the formation.

Emil

E mil was checked out in most of the Luftwaffe's aircraft but he was not as-signed to a fighter unit. Because of his experience, the base commander or-dered him to fly as wing-man to Kurt, the *Staffel* commander. The base com-mander was certain the old fox could handle himself in any situation. Emil had already flown so many types of aircraft that no one bothered to ask him if he knew how to fly this one. The Luftwaffe did not feel the need to use checklists. They felt that a good pilot should always be able to remember all the proce-dures.

They gleefully ignored the crashed airplanes lying around the perimeter. So what if a pilot forgot to lower his landing gear before landing—Hitler was mak-ing lots of new airplanes. Flying was dangerous, but also very exciting.

Emil carefully went through a checklist from memory and started the en-gine without any problems. He wasn't sure of the takeoff speed but stayed with the flight leader and climbed happily up to the proper altitude.

Emil noticed that the controllers were having problems locating the bomber formation. Confused fighters were circling without any sighting of the enemy. The experienced pilots were uneasy and did not like flying without di-rection.

The bomber formation was fortunate that the Luftwaffe fighter control was confused, and they reached their target without receiving any organized at-tacks. Most of the attacks were by single fighters easily discouraged by the vol-ume of the fire from the bombers. The flak was light as they turned back to-wards England. No one dared relax while they flew over France, but some of the young gunners decided to stop worrying about the enemy and were starting to day dream.

Kurt

K urt, the *Staffel* commander, was frustrated because he had not been able to intercept the bomber formation. He decided to follow it to England. When they crossed over the familiar English coast, Emil realized that this was breaking his rule of not taking stupid chances in combat.

He was just starting to close his throttle and head for home when his commander made the same decision after seeing the sky full of Ami airplanes, and ordered the *Staffel* back to home base. Some of the younger pilots swore under their breath about their cowardly leaders and stayed behind the bomber formation. One brave young eagle picked out a B-17 that was on its downwind leg in the pattern to land and was certain of an easy victory.

Jim

Jim watched the sky around him like a wary eagle waiting for something to attack. He noticed a single fighter approaching from behind and thought if it was an enemy fighter it would be an *Me-109*. He automatically adjusted the gun sight for the wingspan of that fighter and trained his guns on it. Allied fighters were not allowed to fly near a bomber base that was landing airplanes.

As it approached Jim thought, *I don't know who he is but he is a goner*, and squeezed the trigger.

Jim's pilot shouted angrily, "What do you think you're doing, firing your guns in the landing pattern? We had our landing gear and flaps down ready to land, so we almost stalled."

The officers in the control tower saw a fighter crash close to the field and radioed, "Somebody just shot down a British Spitfire."

Several B-17s saw Jim firing, retracted their landing gear and flew away. When Jim's B-17 turned on base leg for landing, he plainly saw the black crosses on the wings of a crashed *Me-109* laying close to his runway.

Jim gleefully shouted into the intercom, "I just shot down a Jerry 109. Watch out—they are following us home!"

Jim's crew were getting back into the bomber the next morning still tired from the last mission. They just wanted a day off to rest, but the high command was eager to take advantage of the good weather over the Continent. They thought that they could stop the Luftwaffe by destroying the fighters on the ground. Jim's bomber was soon headed for France again.

Werner

Werner was again trying to predict where the *Amis* were headed today. The bombers were in smaller formations and going in different directions. Because the *Amis* had bombed Luftwaffe fighter airfields, he thought he saw a pattern. Maybe they were going to make him defend his airfields instead of bombing factories as they usually did. He looked at his map of Europe with all German airfields marked on it and immediately issued orders to all fighter bases to be put on the highest alert.

Hans

Hans stoically strapped himself into his fighter when the alert was given. He was not with his unit but all pilots and airplanes were assigned to fly anyway. The *Schwarzemänner* had noticed Hans's demeanor and had decided to let him strap himself in.

It wasn't long before he heard the command to start the engines and take off. Hans listened to the controller informing his flight leader that the *Pulk* (bomber formation) was headed toward Paris, France. They would likely bomb any of several airfields around Paris. The pilots didn't care which one once they spotted the *Pulk*. They all found their place in their own formation and wheeled in to attack the *Pulk* head on.

Jim

Jim had spotted the German fighters forming up to attack and alerted his crew. He had a sick feeling in his stomach before he spotted the fighters. Now as they rolled into attack that feeling was replaced by excitement.

He picked out the closest fighter and opened fire. He watched his bullets hit the *Fw-190* in the engine and walk back towards the fuselage fuel tank. The fifty caliber tracers set the gasoline on fire and Jim watched the *Fw-190* explode and spin out of sight.

Hans

Hans had coolly fired his cannon into a B-17. Pieces had flown off of the bomber though it continued to hold its place in the formation. Hans missed colliding with the wing of the bomber by a few feet.

As he pulled up to make another pass he spotted a *Fw-190* crashing in flames. He had no feeling at all for the loss of the German pilot. He didn't know the pilot and didn't care who he was.

He knew that any day he could die the same way. Bombers and fighters were burning and falling from the sky, while parachutes floated down slowly behind the *Pulk*.

Jim

Jim watched the German fighters forming up for the next attack. There were not as many as there had been in the first attack and they chose to attack a flight that wasn't Jim's. A few more B-17s fell from the sky but the bombers dropped their bombs on the Luftwaffe base.

Jim dryly remarked over the intercom, "That will keep the Jerries busy for at least half a day." As the bombers turned back for England they came in range of the German flak guns. Explosions rocked Jim's airplane while shrapnel struck the fuselage. The left wing had a huge hole in it. From his position in the top turret Jim could see the ground through the hole where there had been a wing panel seconds before.

The co-pilot asked him to report on battle damage. All Jim could see was that the cables running through the wing were still intact. Jim asked the pilot how the airplane was flying. Everything otherwise looked all right and they were able to keep their place in the formation. The crew gave a huge sigh when the English Channel appeared through the haze.

Approaching the airfield, Jim told everyone to be on the lookout for German fighters that might have followed them home. The pilots carefully slowed the B-17 down, watching for any sign of damage. The landing gear came down as it should and then they tried the flaps. The wheels shrieked as they touched the runway.

Jim and the rest of the crew quietly picked up their equipment and dropped out of the bomber. They didn't know it then, but they would never fly in that B-17 again. The crew chief inspected the damage to the wing and knew that he would have some long days before he could get that airplane back in the air.

That evening, Jim's crew was certain that they wouldn't be flying the next day. Some even hoped that they might get leave to visit London and be able to sleep in the next morning.

The word was that tomorrow there was going to be a massive raid to celebrate the first anniversary of American bombing of Europe. The navigator and bombardier from Jim's crew volunteered to fly with another crew the next day. They wanted to get their twenty-five missions over with as soon as possible.

The next morning at two a.m. when the crews scheduled to fly were awakened, Jim and his crewmates were told they were also needed. When they complained that their airplane was not airworthy, they were given another older B-17. It was one of the few survivors of the original B-17s that had flown the first bombing mission over Europe.

Jim groaned when he heard the serial number of the bomber they were assigned. Everyone said that this particular B-17 had survived so long because its many mechanical failures kept it from completing most the missions it started.

The sudden change in plans led to many mistakes. Jim's crew was given the wrong parachutes. Jim tried to tell everyone to readjust the parachute harness to fit them. In the confusion, some of the crew didn't get the message. It would lead to an exciting experience for one of them.

Jim and his fellow crew members stepped down from the truck that had brought them to the flight line, expecting to enter their bomber and take off for Schweinfurt. Instead they saw a dense gray English fog engulfing the entire airfield.

The loaded B-17s were dripping wet, water running in rivulets off the trailing edge of the wing. The ground was soggy and as the men breathed in the moist air, they felt as if they were filling their lungs with water. The atmosphere was something out of a nightmare.

The men milled around the airplane smoking, since no one felt like talking. The officers knew from their briefing that they were supposed to take off at 09:45. The Regensburg formations were to be in the air at the same time, splitting the Germans fighters between the two raids.

After a one-hour delay the fog began to disperse and it was not quite so gloomy. Jim watched a farmer arrive in a grain field nearby. Horses were pulling a grain binder. Jim was very familiar with horses and had operated a similar binder at home. He asked the pilot for permission to visit the farmer.

The pilot said, "Sure; I doubt if we even fly today," unaware that the Regensburg formation was already airborne.

Jim approached the farmer with a friendly grin and asked if he could pet the horses.

The farmer replied, "That's fine with me. They're nothing special, just ordinary English work horses."

When the horses saw Jim approaching, they snorted and gave him a friendly neigh as a greeting. Jim had to laugh. He had always had a special affection for horses and it pleased him to think that the English horses would recognize him as a friend. He patted the soft nose of one of the horses. The smell of the horses and the sight of ripe grain gave him a pang of homesickness. Seeing the bombers sitting in the fog and the dismal scene of a military operation, caused him a moment of disorientation and he wondered how he had ended up in a foreign land, about to go in to battle against an enemy that would give him no quarter.

He watched the fog slowly dissipate and with sorrowful good-bye to the English farmer walked back to the waiting B-17.

He had always had a positive outlook on all the other missions but this time it was different. The changed plans, flying an airplane that clearly should have been junked, strangers' equipment and the long delay in taking off made him a little nauseous.

As he approached the airplane he noticed that the crew members had strange looks on their faces. The pilot was missing. Then he heard someone retching behind the tail of the airplane. A few moments later a white-faced pilot emerged.

The crew members looked away in embarrassment, trying to hide their own anxiety. Only the officers knew the details of their mission. The co-pilot stared at the ground in silence. The bombardier and navigator were replacements for the men who would have normally been on this mission. They looked pleadingly at the sky and wondered how they had ever gotten assigned to this crew and to this beat up B-17.

Early that morning when Jim's crew prepared for their mission the radio operator switched on the radios to see if it they were operational. A German radio operator listening to the *Ami* radio frequency heard a click.

As the B-17 radio operators turned on their radios they all clicked in the Germans' headsets. There were so many clicking at once that it was difficult to count them.

The German officer in charge remarked, "*Mein Gott*, I can't believe the Amis have that many bombers." They wouldn't at the end of the day.

The officer immediately called headquarters. The officer receiving the call at first refused to believe the report, remarking that maybe the *Amis* were sending out fake signals to deceive him. After studying the numbers he realized that he had to alert all available fighter units. In the fighter ready rooms all over Belgium, Holland and France telephones were ringing, sending out the alarm.

Kurt

Kurt heard the alarm ringing and slowly stood up to put on his flying gear. He was still sore from his latest wounds and was looking forward to a day off so he could relax. As his head cleared he was at least reassured remembering how well the new tactics were working.

The younger pilots were learning how to attack and the ones who did not have the nerve to follow through had been sent to other duties. The pilots who had learned the frontal attack soon realized that as dangerous as it appeared, it was nothing like attacking from the rear at slower speeds. Those who tried the rear attack didn't do it again.

The only protection the B-17s had in front were twin guns in the top turret. They had a longer range than the twenty-millimeter cannon but the cannon had more firepower. The German pilots liked to begin their turn toward the bombers at least two miles in front of them. Lining up on a moving bomber bouncing in the air was not easy.

By now the German listening posts could hear the garbled conversations as the bombers went airborne and formed up for the raid. The Regensburg mission was headed for Germany. The Schweinfurt B-17s were still sitting on the ground, dripping wet from the thick fog.

The fourteen cylinders on the BMW engine were already coughing and the engine cooling fan howled in protest as Kurt strapped himself into his airplane. He plugged in his headset and listened to an excited controller giving out instructions. The controller paused for a few moments, then shouted, "*Alle Maschinen starten—mach schnell.*" (every machine start and take off immediately) Kurt released his brakes and applied full power to the BMW engine. His fighter jumped forward and was immediately airborne.

Emil and Kurt

Emil had heard earlier that the Luftwaffe was expecting a large bombing raid today. He had five years of aerial combat and knew from the harried expression on the faces of the staff officers that something big was about to happen.

He knew from experience that when the call came to take off, he did not want to run a long distance. So he was standing next to his *Fw-190*. He was not an officer and as a senior sergeant he was able to communicate with the crew chief about the condition of his aircraft.

It was important to him to know what problems might arise in the air. He hoped that his engine wasn't an old one with major problems. The crew chief proudly showed off the repaired bullet holes like they were major victories for the ground crew. Emil had just been assigned to the *Staffel* and was acquainted with very few of the personnel. Not a problem, since he was used to getting thrown into bad situations with little or no notice.

Emil hated the wait before take-off. For most of his other assignments he had a designated starting time. He always felt better when he was sitting in the cockpit. This time he decided to get into the cockpit before the alert call came.

He had just fastened the straps to his seat belt when he saw the other pilots running for their *Fw-190s*. His mechanic frantically signaled for him to start his engine, the propeller turned through several rotations and started with a loud roar. He saw Kurt's fighter taxi past at a high speed.

Emil released his brakes and followed him to the end of the runway. After take-off, he put his left wing right beside the leading *Focke Wulf*. The rest of the *Staffel* was strung out behind the two leading fighters.

Kurt wasted no time waiting for the rest of his *Staffel*. His tactic was to climb as high and fast as possible. He needed to gain enough altitude so that he was above the bomber *Pulk*. He also wanted to position everyone so that they could attack the *Amis* with the sun at their backs and in the *Ami's* eyes.

Once he had the right position, Kurt started circling to allow the rest of the *Staffel* to form up. Kurt felt confident that he was in position to make a perfect attack. He had at least eight *Fw-190s* perfectly lined up for a head-on attack.

Emil had to laugh when he saw the number thirteen on Kurt's *Focke Wulf*. The big numbers were inviting the enemy to attack. No wonder he had been shot down so many times. Rumor had it that a Luftwaffe fighter, after seriously damaging an *Ami* bomber, had escorted it to a landing on a German airfield. No one in the Luftwaffe ever reported it. And it seemed that Kurt had done it more than once.

Emil had no problem flying at high altitudes. He had flown at forty thousand feet many times. You just didn't want to make any quick moves. He was impressed by how well some of the less experienced pilots performed in such a chaotic combat situation. His *Staffel* was well positioned, up sun. They were the proverbial, extremely dangerous *Hun in the sun.*

American B-17 Regensburg attack

The Regensburg formation of one hundred thirty-nine bombers crossed the Dutch coast at 10 a.m. The foggy weather in England had delayed the Schweinfurt raid. The plan was that the two raids would cross the coast of Holland simultaneously.

It was hoped that the combined raids would overwhelm the German fighters. The American fighters could only escort the bombers as far as Eupen, Belgium on the German border. Then the bombers would be prey to German fighter attacks. Number thirteen was circling high above them with the sun at his back.

Hans

Hans was now considered one of the more experienced fighter pilots. He had already fought and shot down several enemy airplanes. He no longer felt elation at his victories. It was not the challenge that he had felt at the beginning of the war. He did not have many friends; he had seen too many of his fellow pilots die and did not want to be close to anyone.

When he had first been told they were going to attack the bombers head-on, it sounded crazy. But after trying it once, he was confident that it was the right way to attack.

His *Staffel* was alerted that a big raid was in the air over England. Hans felt nothing and talked to no one. He impassively watched the other pilots talking excitedly with each other. He was certain that he would not survive the war.

Still, when an adjutant stepped into the ready room and announced in a loud, professional, Prussian voice, "*Alle Piloten starten sofort.*" (all pilots take off immediately) a rush of adrenaline shot him out the door towards his fighter.

The adjutant shouted at the running pilots, "I hope you find enough targets today!" Little did he know how many they would find!

When Hans started the large BMW engine on his fighter and felt it shudder like it couldn't wait to be airborne, a wave of excitement rushed through his body. The thought did enter his mind that today could be his last day on earth. He waved to the crew chief, something that he normally didn't do.

The crew chief just looked at Hans and thought, "I wonder how much he drank last night."

Werner

Werner had received prior notification that a large raid was on its way from England. The German radio listening posts had heard the *Ami* radios turning on. When he asked how many there were he was told more than they could keep track of. He had immediately given the order to alert all fighter units.

Werner studied all his maps trying to guess what their targets might be. He was surprised at how long it was taking to assemble their formations. At last the German radar began to pick up the image of a large formation headed towards the Dutch coast.

As German radar began to pick up on the bombers on their screens, the American general on the Regensburg raid was watching his bombers emerge from the clouds. The commander was elated when he saw every airplane take its proper place in the formation. He shouted at his pilot, "All that training paid off; not a single collision."

The most dangerous part of the bombing mission was taking off in fog while overloaded with bombs. Avoiding collision with another bomber took skill that could only be acquired through hours of training. Now a formation of B-17s twenty miles long approached the coast of Holland.

Werner had six *Gruppen* of fighters either in the air or approaching the bomber formation. He didn't know the bombing target but knew that there were too many bombers in that formation for it to be just a diversion. He now had one hundred fifty fighters available, and they could all stay in contact with the bombers for thirty minutes.

Kurt

Kurt was still circling with Emil close on his wing. Now he was receiving reports on the location of the *Pulk*. This enabled him to keep the sun behind him and in the eyes of the bomber crews.

Radar reported that the *Ami* fighter escort was turning back. They didn't have enough fuel to accompany the bombers all the way to their target. Kurt was surprised at how fast the bombers were approaching. Kurt could see the bombers and realized he would have to act now or lose his advantage of attacking from the sun. Kurt's *Focke Wulf* gracefully dipped its left wing and dove at full power into the formation.

Jim

Most of the men on the Schweinfurt raid believed that their mission would probably be scrubbed. They had already been up for a long time and were starting to feel hungry. Jim was already exhausted. His crew had flown missions the last two days.

Now jeeps were moving through the parked bombers while men in the jeeps shouted at the lounging crews to start their engines. Jim's crew simultaneously groaned as they reluctantly pulled themselves into the belly of the bomber.

Jim positioned himself standing between the pilots. He watched their every move as they went through their checklist. He did not like to fly the older bombers. This had been one of the first B-17s to arrive in England.

All the engine instruments moved into their proper places, into the green. A flare popped into the sky, burning a hole in the fog. A B-17 sitting on the runway roared as the pilot applied full power to its four engines. With a full load of fuel and bombs it moved very slowly at first, finally reached its takeoff speed and staggered into the air.

Jim's pilots had taught him how to fly the B-17 after hearing reports of flight engineers flying a damaged bomber home when both pilots had been killed. As Jim's airplane started its take-off roll he was pleasantly surprised to hear how smoothly the engines ran.

Jim watched the airspeed indicator and then started giving the pilots a running commentary on their speed. The B-17 bellowed and bounced as the airspeed rose slowly. Both pilots watched as the distance to the end of the runway shortened. At the last moment the tired B-17 attained enough lift to fly—just enough. Jim let out a sigh of relief and remarked over the intercom, "That was close enough to make a man swallow his chewing tobacco!"

Emil

While the Schweinfurt raid was still preparing for takeoff, Kurt was attacking the Regensburg formation. Emil stayed with his commander throughout the dive. Now at a combined speed of five hundred miles an hour they headed straight for the lead bombers, flying through a shower of fifty caliber bullets.

Emil fired a short burst of twenty-millimeter cannon fire that splashed across the wing of one of the B-17s. He sailed through the formation, spotting number thirteen ahead and above him. Kurt was climbing and turning back toward the bombers at full power, racing to get ahead of them so he would be in place to attack again.

Emil's reaction to his first attack on the *Vier Mots* (four engine bombers) was that this was a very dangerous way to make a living. He might need to rethink his plans for surviving the war.

He watched two of the bombers catch fire and drop out of the formation. White parachutes floated behind the stricken B-17s. At least some of the crew were getting out. Emil had no idea which bomber he had attacked.

He closed up on number thirteen and watched as they passed the bomber formation. They needed to be at least two miles ahead of the formation before they turned for a head-on attack. No more than half of the original *Gruppe* had followed number thirteen for the second attack. Emil thought, *it's going to be more exciting this time around!*

Hans

Hans took off as quickly as possible and hurried to get in the proper position to attack the Regensburg formation. The BMW engine was at full power while he tried to gain as much height as possible. Ground controllers gave him the *Tampen und Kirchturm* (course and altitude) of the bomber formation. Other units had already attacked the formation and Hans heard cries of *"Horrido"* as German fighters downed several bombers. Soon Hans could see the smoke of the crashed bombers; the formation was just ahead of the wreckage. Hans' *Gruppe* was able to attack with plenty of height and with the sun at its back.

Hans was now in his element, confident that he could bring down the bomber he was attacking. Even at the high closing speed Hans thought that this was going to be a perfect attack. The pilots in the B-17 had no protective armor in front of them.

His twenty-millimeter cannon coughed out several shells and both pilots died instantly. As Hans flew through the formation he did a slow roll to mock the bomber crews.

After a quick look at his fuel gauge he reduced power and looked for the nearest airfield. His engine burned a lot of fuel at maximum power. When he landed, he spotted several of his fellow pilots.

One said he had seen the *Vier Mot* Hans had been shooting at crash. He felt nothing, but his comrades all congratulated him on his success. The route to Regensburg was strewn with the burning wreckage of crashed *Ami* bombers, one of them smoldering a short distance from Worms, Germany where Martin Luther had started the Reformation.

Werner

Werner realized by now that the obvious target was Regensburg. He could see very clearly the track the bombers were taking. The Messerschmidt factory was located in Regensburg. The Amis wanted to destroy the *Me-109s* before they were built.

Most of Werner's fighters were on the ground refueling. They were strung out in airfields all along the Rhine. Werner was content in the knowledge that they were in a perfect position to attack the Regensburg raid as they returned to England. If the *Amis* had paid a big price getting to Regensburg they were going to pay a bigger price when they flew back to England.

He was receiving reports from a Luftwaffe *Me-110* that was following the B-17 *Pulk*. Instead of turning back to England they were flying south. What were they doing? Werner had no fighters stationed that far south. Had the *Amis* outsmarted him? Did they plan on changing the way they flew their missions?

Werner had his fighters waiting on the ground in what seemed like the perfect position. He had ordered other more distant units in the direction he guessed the *Pulk* would go.

Did the B-17s carry enough fuel to fly to North Africa? One of his brothers was already flying to get a part of the action. Was he too late?

Now Werner received the report that an even bigger *Pulk* of *Vier Mots* was approaching the coast of Holland. They were following almost the same route as the previous raid. That meant that their fighter escort would have to turn back at Eupen and the *Pulk* would lose their protection.

Were they crazy? Did they have so many planes and crews they could take impossible loses and still get through to bomb their targets? It appeared so. This wave was four hours behind the Regensburg raid. That would give the Luftwaffe pilots time to eat and relax, refuel and rearm their fighters.

Emil and Kurt

As a second, smaller wave of fighters attacked and the B-17s' fifty caliber machine guns found the range, Emil thought it was like flying into a snowstorm, except the snowflakes were made of lead. In the second that he had to fire he struck an outboard engine on one of the bombers. He followed number thirteen through the formation. Looking back, he saw two of the bombers slowing down and dropping out of formation.

Kurt flew east and started to descend; they were almost out of fuel. Entering the landing pattern at a small airfield, they landed behind several fighters from their *Staffel*. The ground staff were scurrying around trying to refuel and rearm the fighters as fast as possible.

Feldwebels shouted *"Mach' schnell!"* Everyone thought that the Regensburg raid would be returning soon on their way back to England. But by now the Regensburg bombers were flying unmolested over the Swiss Alps on their way to North Africa.

Schweinfurt raid, American B-17 crew

Jim was like a mother hen watching over her chicks. He checked to make sure everyone heard the commands given by the co-pilot. He listened carefully to the answers given by the crew. The pilots were too busy to think of anything but flying the airplane and keeping the airplane in formation.

The navigator was staring in disbelief at his map. He plotted their course and realized that they were going to fly a very long mission, all of it over enemy-held territory. He saw that they would be exposed to attacks from the Luftwaffe most of the way and without a fighter escort for the greater part of it. It looked like a suicide mission.

For the navigator it was. He was tired and indifferent. He had not been scheduled to fly today and was upset when he had been awakened at two a.m. that morning and assigned to a strange crew to fly a mission in one of the oldest B-17s in England. Or maybe he knew that it would be his last day on earth.

The bombardier had even less to do until they reached the target. He had also not expected to fly that day but reluctantly did whatever came his way. He was not impressed with his crew and when the pilot had lost his breakfast behind the tail of the bomber he knew it was going to be a very long day.

Jim listened carefully when the co-pilot gave the order to put on oxygen masks and made sure that everyone's oxygen system was working. He worried about the indifference shown by the waist gunners but the other three men were all competent and could be counted on to do their jobs. He was going to get to know them much better over the next two years.

When they'd first arrived in England, the pilots had listened to those with more experience tell them what was likely to happen to them. The pilot had decided that it would be important to teach the flight engineer how to land a B-17.

The staff officers would have been outraged if they'd heard about it, but it was not that difficult to make sure that the staff did not know about it. Many crews were doing the same thing. Anyway, Jim had enjoyed flying the big bomber and had felt confident that he could land it in an emergency.

Jim's bomber was over the English Channel and the co-pilot gave the order to the gunners to test fire their machine guns. Thousands of rounds of fifty caliber bullets would fall harmlessly in to the sea, as two hundred thirty-one bombers tested their guns.

Jim set his gun sight for the wingspan of the *Me-109*. He would probably only need to worry about them or the *Fw-190*. They were easy to tell apart because one had a pointed nose and the others was blunt and rounded. He liked to have his guns charged and sights set for any possible attack. He was not going to let even a friendly fighter come too close.

Jim was now sitting in his turret, continually turning around watching for enemy aircraft. He felt like he was on top of the world with the blue sky around him and hundreds of large American bombers thundering through the sky. He realized that he was part of a huge armada making history.

He saw their escort of American P-47s weaving above the formation. He was happy to see them but did not want to think about what would happen once they had to turn back. He didn't know all the details of their mission, but he did know that they were carrying a full load of fuel. That meant they were in for a long trip and would certainly face plenty of Jerry fighter attacks. His group was in the high lead group, so he could look forward to being one of the first attacked.

Kurt and Emil, Schweinfurt raid

Kurt, with Emil flying on his wing, was once again circling in the sun with his complete *Staffel*. The only difference was that now, four hours later, the sun had moved further west and the Amis would see them sooner.

Kurt said, "*Es macht nix*." (it doesn't matter) We are going to attack anyway."

Hans

Hans was already climbing to gain altitude for the next attack. Like everyone else, he wondered why the *Amis* were flying almost the same route that they had flown earlier that day. What kind of men were flying these bombers? Maybe they were paid mercenaries. Why did they want to bomb Germany anyway? Whatever their reasons, he would make them pay a high price.

American B-17 crew, Schweinfurt Formations

Jim watched as the escorting fighters turned back to England. He did not feel good about this mission. Nobody liked the fact that they had been assigned to fly it at the last moment as an afterthought by some brass hat.

From his position on top of the bomber Jim could see the patches that had been used to cover the battle damage from previous missions. The pools of oil under the engines had not helped his confidence either. Then to make matters worse, they had been given another crew's parachutes. Jim had told his crew to remember to adjust the harness to fit properly. They all reluctantly agreed though some promptly checked their chutes. Both waist gunners nodded and looked the other way. They had both agreed that they would never jump from an airplane with or without a parachute.

Then there was a four-hour delay. The officers knew that they should have started with the Regensburg raid. That was probably why the pilot was vomiting his breakfast out behind the airplane.

When they crossed the coast of Holland, Jim checked the time: fourteen hundred hours. They had been awake exactly twelve hours. Jim had eaten a good breakfast, but many in the crew were too nervous to eat. They had at least eight hours of flying to go. Five of the crew would never eat another meal while the other five would soon be eating foreign food.

Jim kept his turret swiveling but spent most his time watching the edges of the sun. Jim reminded the gunners that they would be fighting for their lives any time now. Then Jim spotted the dark shapes lining up to attack them. He was ready.

"*Fw-190s*," he shouted into the intercom and quickly adjusted his sights for the wingspan of the stub-nosed fighter.

Kurt and Emil

K urt could see that this attack was going to be different from the earlier one. There were even more bombers and already he could hear the flight controllers bringing in more fighters.

Emil could see the huge formation of B-17s with the Rhine River in the background. The sight of a monstrous armada of invading enemy moving over a serene German landscape was enough to enrage the most peaceful person.

Racing towards the invader he picked a bomber towards the back when he saw most of the gunners firing at Kurt, his *Focke Wulf* flying through a shower of tracers. Emil thought, "No wonder this *verrückter Kerl* (crazy man) has so many wounds."

Emil fired at the left wing of the bomber, some of his cannon fire hitting the inboard engine. He hurtled past the stricken airplane and caught a glimpse of number thirteen gaily rolling away from the *Pulk*.

Schweinfurt raid, American B-17 Crew

F rom his perch on top of the B-17, Jim could see a bomber falling, an engine and wing on fire. It would be the first of many shot down that day. It reminded him of an eagle attacking a flock of geese. If he could have listened to the German frequency he would have heard a triumphant cry of *"Horrido!"* Now a second bomber fell in flames. Another *Horrido*, then two more. The slaughter had begun.

Kurt and Emil

Kurt was starting to feel his old wounds, the high altitude and the G forces making his whole body ache. He knew if he was going to protect his homeland he would need to shoot down many more *Ami* bombers.

The bomber formation was moving so fast that he fell too far behind to catch them and his fuel gauges told him to land, *macht schnell*. Kurt waggled his wing and started his descent, looking for the nearest airfield.

Emil followed Kurt's fighter on its way down. He was exhausted and wondered how long he could keep flying without breaking down physically. He could see smoke from downed B-17s smudging the beautiful scenic picture around the Rhine River.

American B-17 Crew

Jim watched another bomber from his formation stagger under a multitude of ferocious attacks. On board were four men on their twenty-fifth mission. They wouldn't survive to rotate home.

Number five down.

Another *Horrido* cry on the Luftwaffe frequency.

As more German fighters swarmed them, Jim could see more B-17s falling out of formation. Many were burning, and since they still carried a full load of bombs they exploded, scattering parts of the airplane and crew all over the sky. He had no time to watch them since seven *Fw-190s* were approaching head-on. He unintentionally shouted over the intercom, "Come on you bastards, I'm ready for you!"

Hans

Hans saw the German fighters swarming around the *Pulk*. There were over two hundred fighters available to attack the *Amis* at this location. He was flying with six other *Fw-190s*. They all attacked at the same time to spread out the machine gun fire.

Hans was flying just to the right of his leader as they attacked the same bomber. He wondered if it might be wiser for him fly a little lower than the leader, so the top turret gunner could not fire at him.

American B-17 crew

Jim had turned his turret so that he could fire straight ahead, seven gray fighters headed straight for him. He picked what he thought might be the leader before the fighter's wing tips touched the lines in his sight. Both fifty caliber machine guns hammered the fighter before it fired its cannon. The engine began to burn, and trailing smoke it began a shallow dive and disappeared behind Jim's bomber.

Hans

H ans saw his leader's fighter taking hits and thought, "*Dummkopf,* you got careless."

No one was firing directly at him, so he had time to aim before pressing the firing button on his control stick. He saw his cannon shells exploding as they walked across the wing of the B-17, struck the inboard engine and exploded into the cockpit of the bomber. He thought he saw blood splatter on the windows as he sailed past.

The bomber immediately started to dive and Hans thought, "Got the pilots for sure."

He calmly transmitted, "*Horrido.*"

The officer listening to the radio turned to his partner and exclaimed, "That was number eleven and we have just started."

Jim

Jim watched his first attacker diving away, and thought, "That is one Jerry I won't have to worry about anymore."

Then cannon shells exploded as they hit his airplane, and the bomber started her last dive. Jim climbed down from his turret to see the headless bodies of the pilots slumped over the controls, pushing the airplane into a dive.

Jim had prepared himself for this eventuality, but he could have never imagined the scene before him. Now he reacted without thinking.

He began the grisly task by unlocking the seat belt holding the pilot's harness. He pulled the body out of the seat.

Wasting no time, he jerked the co-pilot's body clear of the controls. He completed this in seconds, but by the time he had pulled the bomber out of its dive it had dropped ten thousand feet.

The bombardier climbed out of the nose of the airplane and saw Jim flying the airplane, the bodies of the pilots on the floor. Seeing his terrified pale face, Jim yelled at him to bail out. He didn't have to repeat that command. He didn't know how many of the crew were still alive. The intercom was gone, and he had no way of telling them to get out. Jim toyed with the idea of flying the bomber back to England.

Hans

Hans was clear of the machine gun fire from the bombers. *"Ich habe Glück gehabt,"* (I was lucky) he thought, watching some of his comrades' fighters burning with white-hot fire as the magnesium in the skin of their airplanes ignited. As the cold reality facing him sunk in, he exclaimed, *"Die haben Pech gehabt."* (They were unlucky). Hans was right above the Rhine River and could see other Luftwaffe airplanes sitting on a cleared field.

Jim

Jim now had a few moments to think before he realized that the number two engine of his bomber was burning. He knew now that he did not have long to live if he stayed.

He could not read any of the instruments on the panel. He decided to stay with the bomber as long as possible so that the crew members in the back would have time to escape.

It was not long before the flames had crept along the wing towards the fuselage where six thousand pounds of bombs waited to explode. He had no choice but to put on his parachute. The bombardier and navigator must have already jumped because their positions were empty.

Jim would meet the bombardier after they were captured, but the navigator was never seen again.

The tail gunner crawled forward after he felt the bomber go into a dive. Jim could see the radio operator frantically cranking to rotate the ball turret so that the trapped gunner could get out. They were relieved to feel the airplane level out.

Jim saw that both waist gunners were still in their positions clinging to their machine guns. Air leaked in through the many holes in the airplane; Jim yelled and motioned that they should jump, but neither one moved. He turned back to help the radio man with the ball gunner. He didn't need much help; the moment the ball turret was turned to the exit position the gunner popped out like he'd been shot from a cannon and proceeded to put on his parachute. Then he was out the escape hatch in an instant. The radio man and tail gunner pleaded for the waist gunners to jump but the airplane was burning, so the three men exited the aircraft quickly.

Hans

Hans lowered his landing gear and turned on final approach to land. He could see the bomber he had attacked plummeting to the ground with parachutes streaming out behind it.

American bomber crew

The remaining crew members had difficulty separating themselves from belts of ammunition streaming out of the stricken bomber. Pieces of the airplane also had to be cleared as they fell into space.

The radio operator pulled on his rip cord to open his chute. Every time he pulled with all his might all he did was spin. He finally remembered that someone in a class had told him to pull the rip cord straight away from his body. It worked and he heard a reassuring pop as the parachute opened wide.

Now he was starting to slip out of the parachute harness. That morning he had received the parachute from someone much larger. Now he remembered that Jim had told everyone to check their harness, even the officers. Now with superhuman strength he clung to that harness, thinking that after all the horrible things that he had just survived he might yet slip and fall to his death.

Jim moved quickly to the escape hatch. When he released the controls of the B-17, the mangled machine went into its final dive. Jim dropped through the open hatch. He knew how to open a parachute and was very motivated to do it quickly *(macht schnell!)*. He was just happy to be free of the burning bomber.

He jerked the rip cord and the parachute opened with a loud pop. He'd forgotten that he was supposed to free fall away from the airplane. The parachute opened just as the dying bomber exploded. Six thousand pounds of explosives collapsed his parachute and now he was in a slow twisting free fall!

Since he knew how to braid horse hair bridles, he decided he should be able to untangle the lines of his chute. He hardly noticed the sharp pain in his back caused by the chute jerking from the exploding airplane. Now he had an open chute above him and was quietly floating down to earth. He was watching the other parachutes and burning aircraft falling from the sky. There was a continuous sound of gunfire as the air battle continued.

The sky was full of German fighters. Jim saw two *Me-109s* turning towards him, and before he had time to react, saw the blinking fire coming from them as tracer bullets whizzed all around him. He could see the pilots' faces, looking at him they flew past.

Jim laughed and thought, "You bastards missed me." To show them he was still alive he waved as they sailed past. Jim saw his formation of B-17s disappearing over the horizon, Luftwaffe fighter swarming all over them. The German radio waves were full of the victory cries. Jim watched the German number twelve going down not long after his bomber was shot down. Number thirteen also fell from the sky after a German fighter attack.

Jim's other surviving crew members were now landing in the numerous fields in the area, German soldiers running to catch them before angry civilians killed them. The navigator from Jim's crew had already been beaten to death before the soldiers could save him. Now the German Army was quickly rounding up the *Ami* airman as fast as they could. It was *streng verboten* (forbidden) for civilians to kill the enemy soldiers; that was the work of the army.

Now, after surviving a vicious air attack and a descent in a parachute, the surviving bomber crew were going to face an even worse danger. Jim saw that he was going to land in a potato field occupied by several German women harvesting potatoes with a heavy tool that resembled a hoe.

A strong wind filled Jim's parachute, dragging him across the field. Before he could release the buckle to free himself, the women were beating him with their tools.

One *Oma* struck him with a heavy blow to the head, screaming, "*Schlag den blöden Kerl tod!*" (beat the idiot to death).

Jim thought he was a dead man!

Then he saw a German soldier take the tool away from *Oma*, and with a loud voice tell the old women, "*Aufhören, Alte – hau ab!*" (stop old lady - get lost) The women moved away, still screaming at Jim.

Before he could get up the soldiers saw that his flight suit was soaked with blood.

One commented, "This man ist *schwer verletzt*." (badly injured).

Jim lay on the ground with several nervous soldiers pointing guns at him, but he was happy to see them. *I finally have some security in my life.*

He could still hear the women muttering in the background. Two soldiers carrying a stretcher came staggering across the soft ground. They placed him not very gently on the stretcher, wondering how they were going to carry all that weight back to a waiting truck.

Jim had seen the wreckage of his crashed B-17 as he was descending in his parachute. The other crew members were rounded up by the German army and brought to the airfield where *Unteroffizier* Hans had just landed.

Hans

Hans quickly ran over to the stunned *Amis* before a higher-ranking officer could stop him. In broken English he asked, "Were you flying in the bomber with the letters LEO on its side?" When they nodded their heads in a yes, Hans said proudly, "I am the man who shot you down!"

He saw an Eighth Air Force insignia patch on their uniform, walked over to the nearest prisoner and said, "I need one of these," before cutting the patch off. The prisoner was so surprised that he said nothing.

Hans then invited them to follow him. He walked over to his *Fw-190* and explained to them what an excellent airplane it was. They were not allowed to study the German fighter for very long before a higher-ranking officer returned the prisoners to their guards.

Werner

As two sweating and swearing German soldiers carried Jim off the potato field on a stretcher, Werner was ordering more fighters to the Schweinfurt area. He was assuming that after bombing Schweinfurt the *Amis* would return to England.

He now received a report from the *Me-110* following the Regensburg formation that it was still flying south. He had no fighters that far south so there was nothing he could do to stop them. The question was, were the Schweinfurt bombers going to also fly south?

Now just south of Wiesbaden the Schweinfurt *Pulk* had turned east. Werner felt certain that they would be flying back to England after dropping their bombs on their target. While studying his chart that showed the positions of his fighters, he realized they were all positioned to attack the bombers when they turned back towards England.

The *Amis* had given him one victory after another today and none of it had been planned by Werner. When the bomber formation had started crossing the channel this morning he had been completely baffled about their intentions, but now they had made every mistake possible. All he had to do was order his fighter *Gruppen* back into the air.

Dankeschön, Amis. Orders were given to the *Gruppen* in the south to take off immediately. The ground crews had thought that they would have plenty of time to refuel and rearm. Now there was panic; not all fighters could take off together so they would have to attack individually and not as a coordinated group.

Werner had been moving fighter *Gruppen* closer to the Rhine River as quickly as he could. Still, he was surprised to see his brother's *Gruppe* come up on the status board. He notice that when he called them into action they would be attacking the bombers where their escorts of P-47's could reach them.

His first reaction as an older brother was to try and contact his brother and give him a stern warning to watch out for *Ami* fighters. He knew of course that it would not look right if the commanding general was giving his brother special treatment when all of his pilots were facing the same danger. He just hoped that someone in his brother's *Gruppe* was warning them of the danger. Anyway, his brother had already shot down fifty enemy planes, so he should be capable of taking care of himself. Werner had more things to worry about than just one action.

American Bomber Crew

Jim and his crew were loaded onto trucks. They could see their crushed bomber laying on the ground with the bodies of the pilots and waist gunners still inside. Two of the crew had landed close enough to the wreckage to be able to look inside and confirm that all four men were dead. The formation of B-17s was almost out of sight but Jim could just see the fourteenth bomber falling and white parachutes streaming out behind it.

Emil and Kurt

Emil landed right behind number thirteen at an airfield far from where they had started. The propeller stopped turning, and immediately *Schwarzemänner* swarmed over their airplane. Panels were popped open and ammunition placed in the racks. Fuel was pumped in as fast as possible.

Emil and Kurt stiffly stepped of the wing on to the ground. The exhausted Kurt exclaimed, "*Ich brauche einen grossen Schnaps.*" (I need a big shot of Schnaps).

A young officer shouted at them, "*Sie sollen starten sofort.*"

An unhappy Kurt shouted back, "Not all of my airplanes are ready to fly."

The officer replied, "Take off with the ones that are ready and the rest can catch up. It looks like the *Amis* are going to bomb Schweinfurt and then turn back towards England. You will need to hurry to catch them."

Kurt groaned and hobbled to his *Fw-190*. His engine was already blowing smoke out of its exhaust pipe, as Kurt struggled to get on the wing of his fighter. His old wounds ached and his scars itched. He immediately took off, not even looking back to see if anyone was following.

Emil couldn't believe the commands he was hearing. He was used to the Luftwaffe acting in an orderly fashion; it wasn't German to be so disorganized. It was abnormal! He could understand the necessity of intercepting the *Pulk*, but not this way. Anyway, he stayed right behind, Kurt flying at full power, trying to gain enough altitude to intercept the bomber formation from above.

Kurt now could see the flack bursts ahead of him, showing him the location of the *Pulk*. The final stages of his superchargers kicked in boosting his manifold pressure, but he didn't think that was going to be enough to get above the bombers.

He had not used his *Wasser Alcohol Einspritzung* (water/ alcohol injection) in a long time and worried the *Schwarzemänner* had not serviced the system. Now in desperation he called out to the *Fw-190s* following him to start their systems and see if they had enough fluid to operate. Kurt saw his cylinder temperature drop as the cooling mixture was injected. Some fighters dropped behind as Kurt and those with fluid in their systems pulled away.

Kurt could see his hometown of Frankfurt below. He had only a short time to think about his family and friends, who lived there, hoping that were all safe in bomb shelters.

The *Pulk* was now turning north, but Kurt thought they would need to turn further west if they were going to England. He decided that he could cut inside their turn and have time to come out of the sun when he attacked.

The *Amis* were moving much faster now that they had dropped their bombs and had burned up much of their fuel. Still running at full power with water and alcohol injecting into his fourteen cylinders, he saw that he was far enough ahead of the formation to begin the attack. He was certain that there was a good chance to kill another bomber.

Emil stayed with Kurt the whole time, worried that his engine might seize up at any minute. He had had a quick course in fighting the *Vier Mots,* all in one day! Now attacking the bombers seemed much easier. Fatigue helped by blocking out any anxiety that he had felt earlier.

Still, when the fifty caliber tracers started banging on the armor of his *Focke Wulf,* he held his breath while firing his cannon at the big bomber. His cannon shells exploded against the left outboard engine. Emil realized that he again had fired at the engines and not at the *Ami* crew members.

He decided to let someone else kill them once they fell out of formation. He turned vertically to miss the large tail of the bomber and immediately eased back the power on his engine when he saw that the water injection was almost gone. Emil found number thirteen and started looking for a place to land.

Hans

The truck carrying Jim and his fellow crew members was hardly out of sight before Hans was told that he would need to take off with just a part of his *Staffel*. They would get more instruction after they were airborne. Hans had just four airplanes with which to attack.

Hans did not need instructions on how to find the *Pulk*. The black smoke of the German flak guns showed him the way. When he spotted the formation, he saw that it was smaller than at the first attack. There were empty spots in the formation, some bomber engines were smoking and many were damaged.

There were some stragglers following the formation at lower altitude and with stopped propellers. Hans was tempted to shoot down one, but saw other fighters lining up for the easy kill. Hans decided to let the beginners have a try at them. He was certain that he could get his second bomber in one day.

The bombers still were able to throw a wall of fire at him, but Hans found an opening and poured his canon fire right into the cockpit of one of them, killing both pilots.

The big bomber went into a steep dive. Hans' earlier kill had gone into a similar steep dive but had leveled out and six parachutes were seen exiting the doomed B-17. Not this time.

The flaming bomber dove straight into the ground and no one had time to get out. Probably no one in the crew other than the pilots knew how to fly.

Hans didn't turn back. He saw that his cylinder head temperature was far into the red so he cut his power as much as possible. He hadn't used his water injection system. Someone had tried to explain it to him but he did not have time for any extra gadgets and didn't want to know more about his engine than how to start it.

He spotted the large airfield on the Main River - Wiesbaden- he knew that they had one of the best drinking clubs in Germany. He cut the power to the engine and went into a steep dive. Cold air rushing past the hot engine caused some of the front cylinders to crack.

Hans ignored the popping sound though he still heard an occasional crack as he taxied up to a parking spot. The *Schwarzemänner* standing nearby heard another cylinder crack and muttered to themselves they were going to be busy tomorrow.

Hans crawled out of the cockpit and walked directly to the club, deciding that he had done enough for one day, with several bombers to his credit.

Werner

More Luftwaffe fighters were arriving to attack the battered B-17 formation. Twenty-five bombers had already been shot down as German fighter pilots shouted out a stream of *Horridos*. Werner was stunned at how long the *Ami* bombers could stay in the air. Why did they keep on coming after they had suffered so many losses? They had bombed their target and now were returning almost on the same route they had flown in. It was easy for them to navigate because they could see the smoking remains of their comrades' airplanes on the ground.

Werner's staff was already celebrating a great victory. They all thought that the *Amis* would hesitate before trying that again. Werner realized that the bomber formation was entering the area where the American escorts could protect them.

Werner was looking at the future and realized that it did not bode well for Germany. The *Amis* seemed to have unlimited resources.

American bombers returning to England

The returning crews in the B-17s felt like they were flying over their own graveyard. They were relieved when they spotted the dots in the sky that resembled American fighters. Maybe they'd get back to England alive. But right now they needed to deal with many Jerry fighters lining up to attack them.

The Jerries had forgotten where the *Pulk* would pick up its escort. Briefing officers had warned them, but it fell mostly on deaf ears. Every Luftwaffe fighter pilot was thinking that this was the moment that they might shoot down an *Ami* bomber. They had heard all the cries of *Horrido* and wanted to get some of the action.

With their attention focused on the B-17s, no one noticed the P-47s coming from behind. The *Gruppen* leader's *Focke Wulf* exploded in a ball of flame as the fire from eight fifty caliber machine guns tore it apart. The German fighter burned furiously, leaving a trail of smoke and debris before it struck the ground. The stunned Jerries scattered but two more went down before they could regroup.

The bombers kept suffering losses despite the help of the escort. Number thirty-four went down by fighter attack in sight of the Channel. Number thirty-five managed to land in the Channel and its crew survived.

The remaining bombers droned on until they were out of sight. There were no more cries of *Horrido* on the German radio waves.

In England, fire trucks and ambulances lined up on the sides of the runway. Red flares streaked from the landing bombers signaling that they had wounded on board.

Werner

Werner had time to briefly think of where his brother might be right now. He heard the report that *Ami* fighters had arrived to escort the beat-up bombers. He noticed that his celebrating staff had suddenly gone quiet. They all looked away when he looked at them, and some turned pale.

An ashen-faced senior officer approached him and blurted, "*Ihr Bruder ist tot.*" (your brother is dead).

Werner's mind went blank. He had three brothers and now two were gone. It wasn't that long ago that all four of them a played together with model trains. Now all four had been wearing officer uniforms of the Luftwaffe pilot.

His next thought was for his parents. They had struggled to raise a family during the Depression when it looked like there would be no future for them or Germany. His parents were not excited about Hitler and his plans, but the boys couldn't wait to become fighter pilots. Especially once they saw how successful Werner had been, they were sure they could conquer the world. Maybe if he hadn't encouraged them, they would be alive now.

Then he realized if they had not been pilots they probably would have been in the infantry. The truth hit him that there was no way out of this war alive. That was going to be the price for following Hitler.

Now the lively boy they had called affectionately "Grubby" was gone.

Werner had fought in combat for five years and there was no end in sight.

Werner tried his best to keep his composure and command appearance. Tired Luftwaffe pilots were landing at the nearest airfield they could find. Wisely, none of Werner's staff approached him. The battle was over and they could make the necessary decisions on their own. They all felt that they had won a major victory over the *Amis*. But it was too bad about the General's brother.

German Pilots

E mil and Kurt landed at an airfield they had never seen before. After they shut down their engines, they sat very still in their cockpits listening to the ticking of their cooling engines. No one came out to greet them. Exhausted *Schwarzemänner* just stared at the airplanes like they had never seen anything like them before.

When Hans landed in Wiesbaden his first thought was getting to the bar as fast as he could and getting drunk. He was not alone; most of the returning pilots had the same idea. He only wanted to drink and did not want to speak to anyone.

As the bar filled up with pilots talking about the day's fighting, Hans became more interested in listening to their conversations. The ones who were the loudest were easy to discount. So far none of the *Horridos* had been confirmed, so some pilots were claiming bombers for themselves that someone else had actually shot down.

Alcohol made them even braver. The more experienced pilots grew tired of the topic and drifted away.

One of the very drunk younger pilots became irritated by Hans' sullen demeanor, and asked, "Well old-timer, what did you do for excitement today?"

Hans answered, "I shot down three *Vier Mots* and flew three missions."

With a sneer the young pilot said, "Can you confirm that?" as he raised his glass and gulped some more cognac.

Hans reached into his pocket and with an unsteady hand tossed the Eighth Air Force patch at the drunken pilot. "I took that off the flight suit of one of the living crew members, after killing both pilots and two gunners. I landed close to where the *Vier Mots* crashed. I shot it down and six other pilots saw it happen."

The other pilot quickly handed the patch back to Hans and left. Hans shouted to the waiter, "*Noch ein' Cognac.*" (another cognac).

Hans sat quietly holding the patch, wondering about the crewmen he had talked to after he shot them down. He didn't feel sorry for them and he did not have any regrets about killing the other men, since he was sure that the same death awaited him.

He was certain that the Amis would keep sending more bombers and that he would keep shooting them down until they killed him. After another hour of drinking, Hans was still sober enough to realize that he was going to be sick. He had been in this club before, so he knew the routine and headed for the door marked "*Herren*." (Men).

In front of him was a large marble bowl; all he had to do was put his head down, grasp a handle on each side and let the cognac do its job. He did not know that one of the pilots he had killed had done the same thing only a few hours before Hans had killed him.

Hans staggered back to his billet and fell onto his bed. Before he went to sleep, he saw the Eighth Air Force patch lying on the floor. He wondered what had happened to the men who had survived the crash of their bomber only to be captured. *Anyway*, he thought, *the war is over for them, and they will probably outlive me*, and fell asleep.

Captured B-17 crew

In a state of shock, Jim was put on a train with his fellow crew members. He did not know where he was except that it was in Germany. The change from a military base in England to sitting in a foreign train surrounded by German soldiers was very disturbing to say the least.

Strange instructions and people speaking a different language made him wonder if this was just a nightmare that wouldn't end. The scenery was beautiful but did not make him feel better. He didn't belong here.

The flight and air battle and escape from a burning airplane had been measured in minutes, yet it had transported him into another world. His stomach reminded him that he had not eaten in eighteen hours. But it was still the same day.

He saw a young guard staring at the prisoners. The young soldier was thinking that these men did not look like the gangsters the Nazis had said they were. Right now they looked harmless enough. One man had dried blood all over his flight suit. The other men were dirty and in shock.

Jim could feel the train slowing down, the guards started looking out the window, trying to locate familiar signs. When the train pulled into the *Hauptbahnhof* (main train station) in Frankfurt, the guards started shouting "*'raus,*" and pushed the prisoners out the open doors of the train.

Jim didn't know what the guards were saying but decided that he should start learning German. As Jim exited the train he could see and hear a large crowd of civilians shouting angrily, "*Luftgangsters!*"

The guards started pushing the crowd back to let the prisoners through. One of Jim's crew members anxiously asked, "Why are they so angry with us?"

Jim sarcastically answered, "I can't imagine why," his bruised and aching back reminding him of the old women trying to kill him with a big hoe.

The soldiers had fixed their bayonets and succeeded in pushing the crowd back. Jim thought it was ironic that enemy soldiers needed to protect him from their own people.

As they marched down one of the main streets, one of the prisoners gasped. Bodies of numerous American airmen hung on the large gas light posts.

Jim was certain this would be the end of the road for them. He thought it strange, that they would be brought this far just to be hanged.

Instead they were led into a large building and given some weak cabbage soup.

Jim remarked, "Enjoy it boys it, may be your last meal."

One of the prisoners sadly said, "Eating this stuff is worse than being hanged."

The guards moved out of the room, keeping the prisoners in and the angry crowds out of the building.

One of the prisoners said, "Maybe we should try to escape?"

Jim dryly commented, "Yes, then we would be safe in the hands of the crowd out there!"

The prisoners were now exhausted as the day's events overcame them. They had no beds or chairs so they sat or laid on the floor. One of the crew noticed that the Eight Air Force patch was missing from his friend's uniform.

He commented, "Didn't I sew a patch on your flight suit for you?"

His friend replied, "Yep and that red-headed Jerry pilot cut it off a lot faster than you sewed it on."

Bomber airfield in England

When the remaining B-17s returned to their bases in England, the officers on the general's staff could not believe their eyes. Not only were so many missing, but many of the returning Bombers were badly damaged.

Sick with the sight of what had happened, they knew they would need to find some way to justify their actions. Someone was going to ask how they could send their bombers so far into enemy-held territory with no fighter escort.

Werner

Werner's staff added up the number of Ami bombers shot down. After all the fighter Gruppen had reported, they were able to determine that a total of thirty-five bombers on the Schweinfurt raid had been shot down and another twenty-five had gone down from the Regensburg raid.

The Amis had lost six hundred airmen in one day! The staff officers sat in stunned silence when they heard the report that the bombers in the Regensburg raid had flown all the way to North Africa.

The Germans knew that they had achieved a major victory over the Amis, but could not believe that the Americans could sustain such losses over a longer period. The Luftwaffe had lost very few fighters, but there was no victory for Werner and his family.

Jim

When Jim opened his eyes after sleeping that night it took some time before he understood where he was and how he had ended up in this big building. It was a few moments before it registered that he was actually a prisoner of war.

Yesterday's memories came flooding back. He was relieved that the angry crowd was gone. The other prisoners slowly woke. They all had to go through the same experience of trying to adjust to their present situation.

Reality arrived when two guards walked in carrying a large tub of cabbage soup. Some of the airmen tasted the soup and commented, "To think that I complained about the food in the Army."

Jim said, "You better get used to it, it will probably get worse."

It wasn't long before their guards opened the doors to the room. "*Raus, mach' schnell*!" (out, quickly!) they nervously screamed at the prisoners. They were not the same guards who had escorted them in yesterday. Mostly they were very young and looked frightened.

Jim whispered to his fellow prisoners, "These fellows might be Hitler Youth. Be careful not to frighten them. They could start shooting."

As they were led out of the building, Jim glanced down the street and saw that the bodies hanging there yesterday were gone. Had that been just a bad dream?

The place where angry crowds had wanted to kill them was now peaceful with only women going about their shopping for the day.

Jim poked the man standing next to him in the ribs and asked, "Did you see bodies hanging from the lamp posts yesterday when we arrived?"

"You bet I did, and I thought we were goners."

As the prisoners were marched down the street toward the *Hauptbahnhof,* some of the older people started to shout at them. The young guards nervously fingered the triggers of their weapon. An old woman shouted at the guards to shoot the prisoners. The young men looked at their sergeant for orders.

The sergeant yelled at the old woman, *"Halts Maul, Alte."* (shut up, old lady).

Jim laughed and remarked, "Yesterday we were fighting for our lives against some of the most dangerous pilots in the world. Today we are afraid of a German granny who wants to kill us!"

The prisoners were loaded into a waiting train that traveled west along the Main River. Jim observed a large chemical factory on the north side of the river. He said to a prisoner next to him, "That place is a great target for our bombers. They could follow the river and place their bombs right in the middle of it. The bombardier couldn't miss."

The train slowly followed tracks that turned north, following the base of the Taunus Mountains. Jim could see old castles on the tops of the mountains. Small villages were scattered at the edges of the fields and farmers were busy harvesting their crops. He thought of yesterday when he saw the women digging potatoes with the same kind of tool that had been used to beat him.

The train's brakes screeched next to one of the larger towns. It had a few buildings that had once been a factory building rotary engines for the German air force in World War One. Now it would be used as an interrogation center for prisoners of war.

The train's doors slid open and guards with evil-looking sub machine guns, screamed the now familiar, *"Raus, macht schnell."*

The prisoners struggled to their feet and slowly entered a building already crowded with other prisoners. Curious civilians watching the marching prisoners were not as hostile as the people yesterday. Some had seen the big bombers in the distance and because they were so high their sound had not been so threatening.

Some of the older German men had worked in the *Oberursel Fabrik* building during the First World War. The old rotary engines they'd built there were long forgotten. Now Mercedes and BMW made most of the Luftwaffe's aircraft engines while their sons were involved in another World War. They were surprised at the number of prisoners and anxious that the Führer had gotten them into a war they could never win.

Jim was busy studying his surroundings. He wanted to know everything that might help him escape. He quietly spoke to one of the older prisoners,

"You need to keep your eyes open and observe every detail. Our survival depends on it."

The prisoners were soon separated into smaller groups and the officers separated from the enlisted men. The Germans were surprised at how young some of the officers were. They were even more surprised that all the enlisted men were sergeants. It was not long before the guards began picking out individual prisoners for interrogation. Now the crew members were suddenly alone with people they couldn't understand.

Jim swallowed hard as he was led into the interrogation room. An unsmiling German officer sat at a desk and behind him on the wall hung a picture of Hitler. Jim suddenly realized the situation he was in. The picture of the Führer made him want to choke with anger. He had long played the officers versus enlisted men game with the Army, but now to be under the control of a foreign officer was more than he could stand.

The officer peered at Jim with cold eyes and said in a loud authoritative voice, "What squadron were you attached to?"

Barely able to control his temper Jim said, "You Kraut bastards already know that my airplane is lying in a field with the insignia on it. You already know my name, and my rank is marked on my uniform. Serial number and blood type are on my dog tags. I may be your prisoner but I will never quit fighting you."

The interrogation officer watched Jim's clenched fists and blazing eyes, and realized that he could be dangerous. He was sure that he could find another man who would give him information more easily.

A swearing and threatening Jim was ordered back into the room with the other prisoners. One of them asked Jim what was going on.

A nervous guard shouted, "*halts Maul, du Kriegsgefanger.*" (shut up, prisoner of war)

Jim laughed. "Now I know what *halts Maul* means and will probably hear it more than once." He decided it was best to be quiet after that.

After several weeks of interrogation, the prisoners were again loaded on a train and sent back to the Frankfurt *Hauptbahnhof.* This time there was no angry crowd awaiting them, only empty cattle cars. They were crowded into them until there was only standing room.

Some wise guy shouted, "I always wanted a scenic train ride through Germany."

Now they realized how difficult it was going to be as a prisoner for the rest of the war.

Jim thought, *most of my time in the Army has been spent riding in trains.*

During the train ride there was not much time for contemplation. The biggest problem right then was to stay upright and not get trampled. Tempers were short but there was no room to start a fight. The officers were separated from the enlisted men and sent to a different prison camp.

When the prisoners were let out of the train cars, they were a sorry-looking group. Still wearing the same clothes that they had on when they left England, no one smelled very good.

Jim's flight suit still had traces of the pilots' blood on it. It would take a lot of washing to get it clean. Even time would not erase the memory of that terrible event.

Needless to say, their prison camp was a dreary-looking place. The hastily built wooden barracks still had a little of the fresh wood color, but before long would turn gray. A tall wire fence enclosed the area and guard towers were scattered along the perimeter.

Jim and a few of the other prisoners immediately began to study their surroundings. Jim dryly commented, "We're going to need to do a lot of digging to get out of this place."

The prisoners were called into formation, counted and then assigned to barracks. It was a tired and sullen group that picked out a bunk. The wiser ones looked at the location of the stove and tried to find a bunk close to it. Once they were settled in they would have time to reminisce and try to comprehend what had happened to them.

The German civilians had only stopped working long enough to beat up and capture the Ami airmen who had fallen from the sky. It was harvest time and they could not waste time with the war. They needed to get the crops in before winter.

The drone of hundreds of bombers was frightening and the rapid rattling of the fifty caliber machine guns had made them want to duck into a hole somewhere. They anxiously watched when burning bombers fell from the sky and pieces of metal were strung along the ground.

An *alte Frau* surveying the wreckage lying in her potato field shook her head and remarked, "Somebody had better clean up this mess, *macht schnell*."

With quiet efficiency, gangs of foreign prisoners guarded by a few older guards cleaned up the bodies of dead airman. They carefully recorded the information on the identification tags they recovered and packed up the body parts they found.

Others loaded the wreckage of the airplanes onto trucks. A few days after the major air battle the only people to be seen in the fields were the ones harvesting crops. Most of the workers were too busy to think about what they had seen, and if they did, they tried to forget it.

In England bomber airfields, a sad and silent atmosphere had settled quietly over everyone. Many spaces were empty where just a day before a large bomber had sat. Most of the bombers that had returned were seriously damaged.

Those ground crews whose bomber had not returned were helping repair the damaged aircraft. They couldn't help but scan the sky occasionally to see if by some miracle their bomber might suddenly appear over the horizon, lower its landing gear, land with a screech, taxi up to its parking spot and shut down its engines. Then the escape hatches would open and they would see the tired crew drop to the ground and greet them.

There was no time to mourn the dead and missing. No one in England knew exactly what had happened to them. The remaining crew members saw many empty chairs when they walked into the mess hall.

Jim's barracks were completely empty; not one of his crew had returned. In fact, none of his squadron's crews had returned. Jim's bed was just like he had left it. Money lay on the bed across from his; someone had left on it after the last night's poker game. The money and most of the crew's possessions were soon in the hands of the men cleaning the barracks. The Army would generously send Jim's hair brush to his family.

The general in charge of the Eighth Air force likewise tried not to look at the charts on the wall that showed the number of B-17s and crews lost. He could not look out of his window without seeing the empty parking spots. He was already thinking that he would lose his job when word got out about the losses on August 17.

More bombers and crews were on their way across the Atlantic Ocean. Staff officers were busy checking the records to see if there was anything there that could be harmful to their careers. They were sure some of the blame could be placed on men who were shot down. The problem was, they didn't know yet who had perished and who was still alive.

Maybe after the war was over nobody would really care. After making a tragic mistake and causing so many deaths, the planners would soon forget that the cause for the tragic losses was that, without fighter escorts the bombers would continue to sustain huge losses.

German view

The Luftwaffe's success in attacking the Ami bomber formations had given them increased confidence and most of the younger pilots felt that they could continue to inflict heavy losses.

There was no celebrating in Werner's family. Already half of the young men in their family had been killed in the air war. All around them, neighbors were mourning the loss of their young men. The speeches that Hitler gave, telling them that they should rejoice and honor their fallen soldiers and airmen, left a bitter taste in their mouths.

Werner knew that with their victory over the bomber formations, the Amis still had gotten through to bomb their targets. He also knew that the American factories were already building fighter aircraft capable of escorting the bomber formations all the way to their targets.

When he informed Hitler and Goering of these fact, they only laughed and said, "That is impossible; no one can do that."

Then Goering cautioned Werner about disturbing Hitler with bad news. He calmly stated, "I learned that if I want to please him, I only agree with everything he says."

Werner, feeling sick, left without saying anything, thinking of his dead brothers and knowing that the war was lost.

American POWs

Jim and his fellow prisoners now had time to study their situation. The first few days were spent looking at every possibility for escape. Slowly, they realized that the German prison system had been well planned. It would take several months before they could find a weakness in it.

The Germans had no plans that would stop the prisoners from organizing among themselves, failing to realize that the Amis were not subjected to the tightly regimented German system. The prisoners were from every layer of social status. They possessed every profession known to western civilization.

Since the prisoners were all sergeants, the Germans thought they would not be able to function without an officer to lead them. They didn't understand that American sergeants had more responsibility than the German military gave its sergeants.

Jim spent much time talking with all the prisoners and found those who would be willing to try to escape, or at least not cooperate with the Germans. He listened as they talked about their civilian professions. Many of them had worked different jobs in different places and were used to thinking for themselves. Right now they were still stunned and depressed from the violence of being shot down and captured by the Germans.

Jim and the other prisoners were finally adjusting to their prison compound when they were suddenly told that they were going to be moved to make room for more prisoners. Someone in the American high command had decided, after studying the fiasco of the Schweinfurt raid of August 17, that they might have better luck if they tried exactly the same tactics again.

Many in the Eighth Air Force including all the bomber crews were against the idea, pointing out that it would produce the same results as the first raid if they did not have a fighter escort all the way to the target. Some English commanders thought that the Schweinfurt ball bearings were so important to the German war effort that the factory making them needed to be bombed again.

Even before the first raid, the Germans had started to move the factory underground. Even if all the bombers hit the target, they would not accomplish much. The men who would fly the mission were positive it would be suicide. The English were happy that the Yanks were so jolly accommodating while the Luftwaffe quietly waited to show them just how stupid their plan was.

German response to second Schweinfurt raid

The mission started as planned and the Germans didn't need to do much differently. The Luftwaffe had all the operations in place to intercept any bomber formations. They waited to see when the fighter escort turned back, which was the same place they had turned back on the first Schweinfurt raid: Eupen, Belgium.

Kurt was waiting in the sun in his favorite spot with his *Gruppe*. Hans was still on the ground but waiting for the alarm to go off. He was nursing a hangover, but that was usual for him. He knew that the minute he was flying he would turn his oxygen to one hundred percent and that would clear his head.

Emil was leading a *Staffel*, which was unusual. A *Feldwebel* did not normally lead a Staffel but because the Luftwaffe had lost so many officers they were using experienced *Feldwebels* instead.

Macht nichts - Emil knew how to teach and lead. Right now he was worried as he watched his *Staffel* attempt to hold their position in formation. Not only were they new to flying, they were headed into combat with the *Ami Vier Mots*. They heard ground control giving them instructions, telling them the *Tampen und Kirchturm* (course and altitude) of the *Pulk*. The young pilots were shocked when they saw the vapor trails of the B-17s. They had never seen that many airplanes in the air at one time and they were supposed to stop them?

It was routine for the Luftwaffe. The *Ami* fighter escort turned back at almost the same place as the first raid. The only thing the German commander didn't know was if the bombers were going to fly to Africa or back to England.

Kurt led his fighters head on into the bomber formation. Several bombers dropped out and fell burning from the sky.

Hans did what he had done several times before and another bomber fell from the sky with both pilots dead.

Emil patiently managed to herd his group of beginners into the proper position to attack. Emil shot another engine to pieces and that bomber slowed down and dropped back from its slot in the formation. Emil again decided to let someone else kill them.

Two pilots who had attacked the B-17s before were able to score. Some o the beginners managed to attack without getting shot down. Several broke of their attack the moment that the fifty caliber bullets from the bombers pelte them.

They were fortunate that Emil was leading them. He took care to gather hi scattered *Staffel*, but by the time they were collected, the bomber *Pulk* was to far ahead for them to attack again. Live to fight another day, was Emil's motto He could hear fighter control giving the *Tampen* and *Kirchturm* of the *Pulk* to other fighter *Staffel* so he led his shaken pilots to land at the nearest airfield.

For the *Amis*, it was the same sad story as the first Schweinfurt attack The remains of sixty more B-17s lay smoldering on the ground with their dead crew members still inside, the prisoners were being led away with the civilian screaming at them. The airfields in England had more empty spaces to bring ir even more bombers and crew to try again.

American POWs

Jim was back on a train again crammed into cattle cars with a large group of *Kriegies* (POWs). It wasn't a long trip but very cold. It was now November and they were going to Austria. Snow blanketed the ground and the gray barracks looked even colder. No one complained as they were led into the prison compound.

Everyone was depressed and tried not to think about their situation. Jim realized that he did not dare show that he felt as bad as the rest of the *Kriegies*. He had to keep up his morale and continue to show a fighting spirit. The first order of business was to keep everyone busy. Then they needed to be organized. Everyone was given a responsibility aside from the work the Germans forced them to do.

After a short time Jim and several older sergeants realized that there was a pool of men trained in practically every trade and profession. Most of the men had lived through the Great Depression and were used to hard work.

Once the men had accepted their situation, they started to plan ways to escape. Every man had a scheme that included using his particular skills. The leaders had to determine which schemes were practical.

The Germans' plan to manipulate the *Kriegies* did not take into account the Americans' independent way of thinking. The Germans had a good system that might have worked if they had not needed to use their less competent soldiers as guards. They did not feel it necessary to use good officers to run prison camps. Old men were good enough for guards because there was not much physical work involved and even untrained men could do the work.

The *Kriegies* soon spotted the weakest guards and began to make frequent contact with them. The guards realized that they were almost as trapped as the *Kriegies*. They were all caught in a totalitarian system using them to further its control of Europe. The *Kriegies* noticed that the guards did not live that much better than they did.

Most of the *Kriegies* realized that it would be useful to speak German so that they could better understand the guards' conversations. Jim had his first lesson in the German language as soon as they arrived in their first prison camp.

He was alone in the barracks when a young guard arrived and shouted, "*Lichter aus!*" (lights out) Jim had shrugged and grinned until the guard smashed the hand resting on a footlocker with the butt of his rifle.

He now knew what "*Lichter aus,*" meant and for the rest of his life never had a strong grip with his right hand. Anyone that worked with him soon found out that the minute he picked up a hammer, you wanted to be out of his line of fire!

Werner

Werner was sitting at his desk when an orderly brought him the reports of the Ami losses in airplanes and happily said, "We really beat up the Eighth Air Force again on that Schweinfurt raid."

Werner only sighed and reached for the reports.

The orderly was surprised that the general was not happy with the numbers. He loudly exclaimed that sixty *Vier Mots* were destroyed in the air and many more were damaged so badly they would probably never fly again.

Werner made no comment but thought, "They will just bring in more airplanes and crews. Now we have thousands of *Kriegies* to take care of, and yesterday we took losses in experienced pilots we can't replace."

Already he was hearing the complaints from his *Staffel* and *Gruppen* commanders that the replacement pilots they were receiving were not ready for combat. They were asking Werner, "How can we train these new pilots and continue to fly combat nearly every day?"

Werner knew that the replacement pilots were only receiving half of the flying time that Ami pilots got before being sent to combat units. None of his superior officers would listen to his warning, least of all Goering and Hitler. After dealing with the German High Command for so long he realized that they knew as much as he did, but did not want to deal with reality.

Kurt

There was not much time for the Luftwaffe pilots to rest. Kurt had to regroup his command. He and the other commanders kept studying tactics about attacking the *Vier Mots*.

Werner their commanding general, could not get Goering to read the reports about the American aircraft production, but he could inform his fighter pilots about what was coming their way. He didn't want to frighten them but they needed to know so they could be prepared for what was coming.

Kurt could only mutter and curse when he flew with the newly trained pilots sent to him as fighter pilots. They could fly an airplane but were at least one hundred hours short of flying a fast fighter. It would take another year to teach them how to attack a *Vier Mots* head on.

Kurt had always tried not to finish off a damaged enemy but give them a chance to surrender. Now, looking at the young men he was going to send into combat with little chance of surviving he was devastated.

Emil

Emil had been sent to command a *Staffel*. Normally that was a position for an officer. Since the Luftwaffe had lost so many pilots after five years of combat, they did not have enough experienced officer pilots so they were forced to turn to experienced *Feldwebels* to do the job.

That some *Feldwebel* would be leading officers in combat caused a major crisis with the higher-ranking officers. The general of the fighters had trained with Emil and knew that if he were an officer he would be leading at least a *Gruppe*.

The general also knew that on the Russian front, the pilot with the highest number of kills always led, and often he was a *Feldwebel*. So he just never let Goering know that Luftwaffe pilots were ignoring rank and letting the most capable men lead in combat. Anyway, *Feldwebels* were much cheaper than officers.

Emil was a good teacher and had survived five years of combat with his philosophy intact. He was always analyzing each situation and studying the possibilities for success. Until now it had always worked for him. But it was going to be very difficult to stay within the boundaries he had set for himself.

The younger pilots were thoroughly indoctrinated with the Nazi idea that they were better than other nationalities. He carefully studied each one to find out their political views before accepting them. He did not want an informer in his unit. He realized that some of the men really wanted to fly and were naturally better pilots. He started training the ones who would learn the fastest, hoping that they could teach the rest.

Emil was not a large or boisterous man, but possessed a soft voice combined with an indignant look that could have frightened Hitler. He quietly explained to his pilots how important it was that they follow his instructions to the letter. Not only did their lives depend on following his instructions but so did his. And he implied that he would be capable of shooting down anyone who didn't follow his orders.

As training progressed Emil only entered combat with his best students and then they only attacked when they were certain of victory. When the pilots realized that they did not have to face combat before they were ready, they gained more respect for Emil.

When his students failed to bring an airplane down, Emil would demonstrate the proper way to do it. His score of kills climbed steadily and stayed even with Kurt's, even though he credited most of his kills to the other pilots.

Kriegies

J im and his fellow *Kriegies* soon settled into a monotonous routine. It gave them time to think about how to escape. Everyone had an idea on how to do that though they were mostly impractical. Before long they picked a committee of men with practical experience in different areas and began to sort out the possibilities.

They had lots of time and manpower. They also realized that tunneling was the only possible way out. Of course the Germans knew that also. The difference was that thousands of *Kriegies* had endless time and energy to plot the best way out, but the Germans had only a few men to guard them.

Hans

Hans was kept busy flying the rest of the year. Someone decided that he needed a rest and sent him home at the beginning of the year. His attitude had not changed since he was still certain that he would not survive the war.

He was not prepared for the attitude of the German civilians toward their military. All the men in his age group were gone, scattered across Europe and Russia. When he asked about them the usual answer was *Tod* (dead) or *schwer verletzt* (badly injured). His mother said that on one list of the killed or missing were eighteen men from her church, all lost at Stalingrad.

What upset Hans was the fact that the civilian population blamed their fighting men and not Hitler -of course no one was brave enough to blame him publicly.

Hans was a loner in the Luftwaffe, but he always knew that the other pilots would protect him even if they didn't like him. He was not the only one who was sullen and angry.

He had always thought in any situation he could find a friend to drink with in his hometown's *Gasthaus*. People he had known all his life nodded a quiet greeting but then turned their backs, afraid to associate with him.

Hans had been drinking heavily for a long time to help handle the pressure of flying in combat. Now the attitude of his countrymen toward the fighting men making all the sacrifices made him even angrier.

He wanted to shout to all these little men, "I hope the Ami bombers blow you away!" Instead, he quietly finished his drink and went home.

When he informed his mother that he was going back to his unit, she silently nodded and sighed. She knew what people in town were saying and she was afraid to talk back for fear of being ostracized by them. She had said nothing when they had cheered Hitler for bombing England.

She was certain that Hans would die in combat like most of the men of his generation. Every generation of German men for the last century had fought in a war. Her husband had fought in the previous war and now her son was involved in one she didn't think he could survive.

Hiding her grief as best she could, she mumbled a quiet, "*Auf Wiedersehen.*"

Hans waved and never looked back. He didn't have any close friends in his unit but at least knew that they were on the same side in this war.

Kriegies

Jim and his fellow *Kriegies* slowly accepted the fact that they were prisoners of a ruthless enemy who would punish them for the smallest infraction of their rules. They also learned that most of their guards were men who were too old to fight, or wounded so seriously that they would not be sent back to the front.

If the guards had ever worshiped Hitler they had quickly changed their minds when they heard the Ami bombs exploding around them. Now instead of conquering the world, they just wanted to survive the war.

It did not take long for the *Kriegies* to discover that they could easily work with their guards, who for a small favor would ignore the rules made by their senior officers. With so many men trying to solve the problem of escaping, plans went forward quickly. Anything that wasn't guarded closely was stolen and hidden for future use.

When the guards were told to search for missing items, they purposefully looked away. They were afraid that Germany might lose the war and having a few Ami friends might be useful in the future.

The *Kriegies* began digging a tunnel under the barracks. Even the laziest of men found the energy to dig when they saw a chance to escape. The men doing the planning soon realized that it was not going to be enough to escape the prison camp; they would need to get to Switzerland somehow.

Werner

Werner was pleased at the number of fighters being produced when he saw the new production figures at the beginning of the year. German factories were doing a great job of producing airplanes in spite of the American bombing.

He had over one thousand fighters available to protect Germany. The problem was that he did not have enough pilots to fly them. Werner had also been informed that the American had twelve hundred fighters to protect another twenty-five hundred bombers now sitting on English airfields.

Also, the new Ami fighters had enough range to escort the bombers all the way to Berlin. He had hoped that the new Messerschmidt jet fighter would soon be available to replace their older fighters. He was just dreaming that he would get enough of them to change the air war. Hitler had his own insane plans and that had already delayed production of the jet.

Kurt

Kurt was exhausted by the number of missions that his *Gruppe* had been flying. The Amis kept coming at least once a week despite the bad flying weather. Many times they were not able to complete their mission but the Luftwaffe still had to try and intercept the formations.

Many of his fighters were flying so much that they were not getting enough maintenance and the engines were quickly being used up. It was not unusual for at least one of the pilots in the formation to make an emergency landing before he could engage the enemy.

Kurt secretly hinted to his pilots to make a bad landing and do some serious damage so they could get a new airplane. If the pilot was killed or injured he could not be so easily replaced.

As the number of his pilots in his *Gruppe* slowly decreased, Kurt knew for certain that the war was lost. All of the violence and killing was just a waste of lives. In spite of his hatred of the war, the number of planes he shot down increased. By the war's end, his kills nearly equaled the number of bombers lost in the first Schweinfurt raid.

Kurt continued to encourage damaged Ami airplanes to lower their landing gear and land at a German airfield, saving them from certain death while taking them out of action as well. Of course the Nazi authorities took no action, because Werner wouldn't tell Goering about these incidents.

Kriegies

Jim and the other prisoners wasted no time once they had a plan of escape. The digging started immediately and with great energy. When the escape committee had a problem that needed a solution there was always a *Kriegie* who could solve it. They even found a solution to traveling through Germany after they got out of the prison. It was not a foolproof plan, but they hoped it would work for some of them.

Jim escaped through the first tunnel built. He managed to stay free for two days before being captured. The guards led him back to the *Stalag* (prison), their dogs encouraging him to behave.

As the recaptured *Kriegies* were returned to the *Stalag*, a dark depression fell over the camp. A few prisoners did not return but no one knew if they had escaped or been killed by the Germans searching for them. Still, after a few days of feeling sorry for themselves, they realized that it was possible to escape.

The *Kriegies* who returned had learned to hate the German guard dogs as much as they hated their human guards. While watching the habits of the guards they saw that the dogs were often left alone outside the prison fence. Everyone agreed it would be a great idea to poison the dogs before their next escape. The escape committee nixed that idea very quickly since they didn't have access to poison. Even if they did poison the dogs the Germans would know that it had come from the *Kriegies*.

Everyone was told to start thinking of how they could eliminate the dogs prior to the next escape. It wasn't long before a prisoner came forward with an idea. He had worked with a veterinarian before the war. A man had brought his dog that had died after eating a piece of cork. When the veterinarian opened the dog's stomach, he saw that the cork had swollen, completely plugging the dog's digestive tract.

The question was, why had the dog eaten the cork? One man said it must have had something on it that tasted good. Another said there were some big corks in the Sauerkraut barrels. They could get plenty of those.

The men working in the kitchen said, "We have bacon grease that would taste good to any dog."

Now the only question that remained was how long it would take for the cork to kill the dog. It was decided to try it out on one dog to find out.

Werner

When Werner saw the combat reports he was not surprised, but only wished they were different. Many of the Nazis only looked at the American and English losses and ignored those on the German side.

It was true the Americans were suffering terrible losses. It was also true that they could afford them with new bombers arriving daily in England.

Werner knew that the Amis were bringing in a new type of fighter that could carry enough fuel to escort the bombers to any target in Germany. Werner had barely escaped them when he flew a fighter to inspect one of his fighter units. Not only did the new Ami fighter have a long range, but it was also fast and maneuverable.

Werner realized that the newly trained enemy pilots were better fliers than the younger German pilots. The Amis were sending more bombers and flying more missions. In February they had flown the most missions in one month since they had started. They had suffered six percent loss in bombers which was less than they had lost in the previous year.

Werner had sent out three hundred and fifty-five fighters to oppose them and had lost one hundred and fifty-five of them. Many of the German pilots had survived to fight again but it was still a heavy blow to the Luftwaffe.

Hans

In his last fight Hans had tried several times to attack the bomber formation but could never get in position before swarms of Ami P-51 fighters attacked him. In a furious fight, his experience and shooting skills allowed him to get off a deflection shot that struck the P-51 in the cockpit and killed the pilot.

The other American fighters respectfully allowed him to escape with a few bullet holes in his FW-190. When he landed, he could see damaged fighters scattered all over the airfield. Ambulances were removing wounded pilots from several airplanes. There were many empty spaces where the Schwarzemänner stood on a parking space, looking into the empty sky waiting for a missing FW-190 to appear. Hans felt nauseated; gone were the days when he had shot down three B-17s in one day.

Now the German civilians working in the fields had to distinguish between the white Ami parachutes and the yellow German ones. They felt better when they saw a white parachute since they could better vent their frustrations when beating up an Ami who had tried to kill them. Some were angry that the Luftwaffe pilot had allowed himself to be shot down.

Hans had always thought that he would die in the war but had been certain Germany would win even if he died fighting. Now the thought that Germany was going to be defeated was depressing.

As was his habit, he left the airfield for the closest *Gasthaus* to start drinking. The next morning, Hans had a horrible headache. His eyes were bloodshot, and he felt emotionally exhausted. He managed to eat a *Brötchen* without getting sick. If he had looked around the dining room he would have seen that most of his comrades looked the same way. The empty chairs did not help anyone's mood.

Hans wanted to start drinking again, but the pilots were told to go to the ready room and wait for the next mission. Hans felt lucky to find a place to lay down and take a nap. He woke when the alarm went off and his head felt like it would explode. He joined the other moaning pilots as they staggered out to their waiting fighters.

He slipped while crawling up onto the wing but managed to catch himself before falling off. He knew the procedure to start the engine by heart and the crew chief helped strap him in. Hans didn't catch what he said, but replied, "*Ja, ja, schon gut,*" anyway.

He managed to close the canopy, had trouble understanding the instructions given over the radio, but just followed the other FW-190s as they taxied to the active runway. Without checking any instruments, he applied full power to the big BMW engine as he climbed into the air. The plane swung to the left, but his many hours of flying allowed him to straighten out before he ran into the prop wash of the fighter in front of him.

His *Staffel* managed to form up into a ragged formation. Someone broke radio silence and said, "I hope the *Amis* are as drunk as we are."

An authoritative voice shouted, "Silence!"

The *Fw-190s* pointed their blunt noses skyward and soon the command was given to turn on their oxygen. With much fumbling, Hans managed to get his mask on. He was surprised how fast his head cleared and the headache became bearable. Now the familiar anxiety started in his stomach and moved up his chest.

The radio was giving instruction on location of the *Pulk* and Hans heard the pilots already engaged in combat. There was the calm voice of the commander and then the excited voice of the younger pilots.

Hans hoped his flight leader felt better than he did. When he spotted the vapor trails of the bomber *Pulk* approaching, he suddenly felt sick with fear, his mind almost paralyzed. He automatically followed his *Staffel* and they formed up to attack the four motor bombers. Someone shouted out over the radio that a formation of *Ami* fighters was approaching from behind.

The commander of Hans' *Staffel* calmly said, "We have time to attack the *Vier Mots* before the fighters reach us."

Numbly, Hans leveled his fighter and headed straight for a bomber, automatically placing the center of his sight on its cockpit. Before he could fire, a burst of six fifty caliber machine gun rounds ripped into his fighter.

His first thought was, "How could the flight leader have so miscalculated the speed of the P-51s?"

His next thought was, "Where is the handle to eject?"

Before he found it, the magnesium in the skin of his airplane ignited and it headed straight down, burning with a bright flame that consumed most of the fuselage and Hans before plunging straight into the ground.

Several burning *Fw-190s* shared the same fate as Hans. The crews in the B-17s that Hans had attacked cheered when they saw the Luftwaffe fighters fighting for their lives. Another experienced *Fw-190* pilot was gone and the odds that the American crews would survive the war had gone up.

Kurt

Kurt had taken off with his full *Gruppe* when the alarm had sounded. As usual, he was climbing with full power to gain as much altitude as possible. He had barely reached his highest altitude when he saw the German black flack bursts and spotted the first bomber formation. Then he saw another, and then another formation coming his direction.

The controller radioed him that the *Amis* had hundreds of bombers in the air and there were fighters escorting them. They were taking a familiar course, flying south with the Rhine River on their left. Kurt could see the Ami fighters swarming around them.

He was still able to fly with the sun at his back. He was sure that they had not spotted him, so at the first opening he attacked. He was able to bring down a bomber but some of his slower comrades were shot down before they could reach their targets.

Kurt was attacked by several angry P-51s. He was able to escape but his *Gruppe* scattered in all directions. He suddenly saw the lead bomber turning east. It was following the Main River and Kurt realized that their target was probably Frankfurt. He had been born in Frankfurt and most of his family lived there. He started to chase the bomber formations, desperate to stop them.

Before he could reach them he could see the clouds of smoke rising from the city, and tons of bombs falling from the bomber formation. The anti-aircraft fire from the ground had knocked down several bombers and the American fighters had shot down many German fighters.

The sky was full of parachutes floating down and pieces of airplanes fluttered as they fell through the parachutes. Kurt was crazy with anger and frustration. One look at his fuel gauges told him he need to land immediately so he found an airfield close to the Taunus Mountains.

As he watched the city of Frankfurt burning below him, his first thoughts were of his family. After landing, he managed to find a motorcycle and raced to see if he could find them.

Emil

E mil hurried toward the bomber formation, his *Staffel* behind him. The controller radio told him that the bombers were headed toward Frankfurt. Most of his family lived close to the city and he was worried about them. He watched as the bombers unloaded their high explosive bombs on his hometown.

He felt rage building and wanted to shoot down as many bombers as possible. He knew that he had survived the war this long because he had managed to control his emotions. Struggling to calm himself, he managed to see that from his present position he would not be able to reach the bombers for a long time. He knew that the bombers would need to turn to the north west if they returned to England.

He ordered his *Staffel* in that direction at full power. When several pilots complained that their engines were overheating, he allowed them to reduce their power setting but ordered them to follow the *Staffel* anyway.

Wheeling around and heading for Koblenz, he spotted the smoke from the airplanes that had been shot down on their flight towards Frankfurt. He had enough time to form his *Staffel* to make a united attack on the bombers. By this time the bomber formations were badly broken up and many stragglers had fallen behind.

Emil could see the twin engine *Me-110s* attacking the stragglers. The anger that had almost consumed him when he saw them bombing Frankfurt subsided, and when he started to fire his cannons he still couldn't bring himself to aim for the pilots in the bomber.

He fired at an outboard engine. Pieces flew off the engine and as the propeller slowed down, the bomber dropped out of the formation. Two more of Emil's pilots shot down a bomber each. The cry of *"Horrido"* rang out, followed by several more as another bomber was shot down.

Emil was drained of all feeling when he landed. A staff officer informed him that two of his *Staffel* were missing and presumed dead. He didn't bother to ask who they were. He was certain that nobody would survive the war; neither the Luftwaffe pilots nor the *Ami* crews.

Kriegies

Jim and his fellow *Kriegies* had been digging like crazy moles. The escape organization resembled a major corporation. The men who did the planning delegated roles to others who then found men anxious to perform the work.

The tunneling was physically demanding. The men digging the tunnel could only work a short time. A pump providing fresh air to the tunnel was built out of scrap lumber. The men working the pump had to be relieved after just a few minutes.

Some men made false passports while others sewed clothes resembling civilian suits. Every trade was represented among the *Kriegies*. The major danger was that the Germans would find the tunnel but fortunately, the prison commanders were not chosen for their intelligence or their integrity.

If they ignored what they suspected was going on they were rewarded with well-behaved *Kriegies*. If they didn't, then they could usually be bribed.

The *Kriegies* had already seen one guard dog die from eating the greased cork. Now they could take out most of the guard dogs when they planned their escape. But they had to wait for a moonless night.

Every prisoner was anxious about the escape and afraid that the guards might sense something unusual going on. If they did, they choose to ignore it.

Not all the prisoners were going to escape, but since Jim had done much of the planning he was going to go out with some of the first escapees. The thought of freedom drove all fear from his mind. He thought that his chances of surviving were better than his chances of surviving a bombing mission in a B-17.

When he stepped out of the tunnel he felt like a new man. His first thought was that he was capable of outsmarting the Germans. He could hear the other men moving around him, but it was not long before all was quiet. Jim was no stranger to the outdoors and kept a straight course for the lights of a farmhouse.

Once he was close he picked another lighted farm and headed for it. He wanted to get as far away from the prison camp as possible before he stopped to find shelter. He was far enough away that he did not hear the sirens going off when the escape was discovered.

Before it was light he found a small barn used to store hay. He hoped the hay would give him enough cover to hide under. He fell asleep but woke up suddenly when he heard a truck pull up and stop next to the barn. He could hear the German sergeant yelling at the men to search the barn for escaped *Kriegies*.

One of the guards who had been raised on a farm, saw a pitchfork leaning against a wall. He looked at the stored hay and thought, "Where would I hide if I were trying to escape?" He promptly started at the beginning of the pile of and stabbed the hay with the prongs of the pitchfork.

Jim heard the stabbing prongs moving closer and thought, "My mother didn't raise me to be that dumb." He jumped up before the startled guard who was more frightened than Jim. In an instant, Jim was grabbed by the other guards and roughly thrown into the back of the truck. He was greeted by several other *Kriegies* who had also been captured.

One of them asked Jim, "What did you learn that would help you if you escaped again?"

Jim irritably answered, "Don't hide in the first haystack you see."

Werner

Werner was having another meeting with Goering. The Fat One started the meeting by acting friendly, but Werner could see that he was quickly turning into his old belligerent self. He had probably been talking to Hitler, was sweating profusely and Werner could smell the fear emitting from the angry, fat man.

Trying to act like one of the most feared men in the Reich, Goering attempted to speak with a deep, intimidating tone, but his voice made only a few squeaking sounds. He lowered his voice and quietly said, "The Führer is very displeased with your tactics in attacking the Ami bombers. He says that the fighter pilots are not aggressive enough in their approach. He wants you to just attack the bomber formation and not worry about their escort."

Werner knew what had happened to Hans and his *Staffel*, but knew better than to argue with the Fat One. He saluted, said, "*Jawohl*," and exited the room. He knew that arguing would only make Goering more unreasonable and Hitler's direct order couldn't be changed.

Werner had not been informed yet of the American and English declaration at Yalta of total war against Germany and Japan. Hitler had always hoped that he might negotiate an end to the war. Now even Hitler's warped mind grasped that he was going to be totally defeated and German cities were going to be bombed into rubble.

Werner knew that his destiny was connected to Germany's and that Hitler was going to blame Goering for betraying him. Despite the sacrifice that the Luftwaffe had made, they would be blamed for losing the war.

Werner had known from the beginning that it would be impossible to win the war against so many enemies. He knew all he could do was make the enemy pay as big a price as possible to win it. The order from Hitler to attack the bombers while ignoring their fighter escort could only be given by someone out of touch with reality.

The Luftwaffe had become adept at ignoring orders from above. Everyone pretended to obey while doing what they knew was best. It would take fifty minutes to form the large formations that Hitler wanted to use to attack the bombers. That meant that the first fighters to take off would have used almost half their fuel before they could attack.

Fortunate for Werner was the loyalty of the Luftwaffe personnel for each other. They had years of experience protecting each other from the Gestapo. They knew how to speak to each other in a manner that an outsider would not understand.

Werner could speak individually to each commander and tell him what Goering wanted and then silently insinuate what he wanted them to do instead. In other words, they would keep on attacking the way they had been. They would use two fighter groups to attack the bomber escort and one *Gruppe* to attack the bomber formations.

The Americans had already bombed Berlin while escorted by the new long-range P-51s. That meant their bombers were capable of bombing all of Germany's cities. It also meant that the Luftwaffe fighters were now going to pay with heavier losses. The Luftwaffe had already lost a third of its fighters while trying to protect Berlin.

Emil

E mil was kept busy herding his *Staffel* through the escorting *Ami* fighters and trying to attack the bomber formations. His years of combat experience allowed him to judge when and where to attack. No orders from a superior could force him into a situation where he could not win.

The loyalty of all the men in his *Staffel* had kept the Gestapo away. The fact that it was impossible to know the exact position of every airplane did not give the officers on the ground any chance to know what was going on in the air.

Emil and his pilots kept radio silence as much as possible so they couldn't have their words used against them. The debriefing officer could only report what the pilots were telling him, plus he was usually part of the team. The *Staffel* was one of the highest scoring in Germany so no one wanted to dispute those figures. But since the *Staffel* was led by a *Feldwebel* the commander was not interested in giving it public recognition.

Kurt

K urt had the same dilemma as all the other Luftwaffe fighter pilots - they were being pushed to their limits, physically and mentally. The Americans were flying daily with higher numbers of airplanes. It was not uncommon to hear air raid sirens every day.

He would sometimes take off with his *Gruppe* to intercept a formation of bombers only to be jumped by hordes of American fighters. The normally calm and collected Kurt would fly right into the middle of the swirling fighters, forgetting the pain and throbbing of his previous wounds.

He still hated killing, but the sight of his hometown being pulverized by the *Ami* bombers caused him to fight regardless of the consequences. The numbers of *Ami* airplanes he shot down continued to rise and at least half were the hated bombers. Still the pressure and conflict with the Nazi political officer watching his every movement made him wish he could be wounded so that he might get some rest in a hospital.

Kriegies

Jim had begun to make plans for the next escape as soon as he was back in the prison camp. Most of the prisoners who had escaped were captured very quickly by the Germans even though they didn't have their dogs to help them.

Some would escape to Spain, but some would be free for several months before they were recaptured. The idea that it was possible to escape inspired the *Kriegies* to begin planning for their next attempt.

Luftwaffe fighter pilots enjoyed taunting the prisoners by flying dangerously low over them. There was always some construction going on in the prison camp so the prisoners collected as many baseball-sized rocks as they could find and placed them at several spots in the camp.

The next time a Luftwaffe pilot buzzed the camp a lucky throw by one of the *Kriegies* hit the propeller of the fighter. The unbalanced vibration caused the fighter to crash into a nearby hillside in sight of the camp. All the *Kriegies* madly cheered as the stunned prison guards watched in disbelief.

The angry prison commandant ordered two machine guns to be installed on the parade ground. He lined up all the *Kriegies* and ordered them to stand at attention for twelve hours. If anyone moved they were to be shot. All the *Kriegies* agreed that the punishment was worth destroying one enemy fighter and pilot. Of course no one ever threw another rock at a buzzing fighter, because none ever buzzed them again.

Werner

Werner was reading reports that showed the overpowering strength of the Americans. He had counted on the Ami's raids slowing down during the winter. They had suffered serve losses during the summer and fall of 1943. He had expected that they would at least slow down to give themselves time to replace their losses. Instead they had flown as much and with as many airplanes as before. Even Hitler had thought that because of the buildup for the invasion they would need to slow down. Now in April of 1944 the Amis had seven fighter aircraft to one Luftwaffe fighter.

When Werner needed to visit any of his units he always flew in a fighter that was fully armed. He did not to trust his life to another pilot. His predecessor had been killed because he was a passenger in an airplane flown by someone else.

Werner was called to Berlin so naturally he jumped into a fighter and headed there alone. He was jumped by several Ami fighters and one had him in his sights. Werner had learned a few tricks over the years and knew from experience that when he fired his guns the smoke would roll behind him.

Hoping to startle the P-51 pilot, he fired his gun and pulled his throttle back. His fighter slowed immediately and the *Ami* pilot flew past Werner, allowing him to escape. The American pilots never knew that they had missed bagging the commanding general of the Luftwaffe fighter command.

When Werner landed he still had to accept that his command had lost so many flight leaders that he did not have enough to cover all his groups. His only solution was to increase the size of each *Staffel* and *Gruppe*.

That was one of Werner's easier problems to solve. Everyone knew that the invasion of Europe by the allies was eminent. No one could mention it for fear an informant or Gestapo agent might hear. Werner wasn't alone in wishing it would happen so that the suspense would be over.

Hitler and Goering had allowed him to bring some units from the east for the defense of the Fatherland but there were at the most one hundred fighter aircraft available to oppose the invasion force. The Amis were still bombing strategic targets in Germany and the Luftwaffe was fighting for its life daily.

There were many contingency plans made to stop the invasion. Airfields had been made for the Luftwaffe planes to operate from and supplies of fuel and ammunition stored there. Unknown to Werner was the fact that allied aircraft were bombing and destroying the airfields, along with the supplies. Communication between The Army and Luftwaffe was almost non-existent. No one in Berlin headquarters knew what was happening. Reconnaissance flights could not penetrate the air cover over England. They could only guess and wait for the invasion to start.

Werner knew that he had only a total of six hundred fighters available and they were scattered all over Europe. The German factories were turning out more aircraft than ever before but the Luftwaffe was losing fighters even faster. Werner did not want to waste much time thinking about it, but he often wondered how someone could be stupid enough to start a war on three fronts and be outnumbered on all of them!

Joachim, German pilot in Russia

In Russia the Luftwaffe was badly outnumbered by the Russian Air Force, but was still a deadly fighting force. Joachim had fought on the Russian front for several years. He had started as a young officer full of energy and enthusiasm and had been toughened by the hardships and heavy fighting. He no longer thought about the politics of the war. He did not need a political officer to inspire him to fight for the Führer.

He looked down on thousands of brown-clad Russian soldier swarming over the steppes, all of them headed towards Germany. Daily he fought the Russian Air Force and was sometimes outnumbered by as much as twenty to one.

He joked to his fellow pilots that there were so many Russian airplanes in the air they had to get in line in order to attack him. It was fortunate that the Russians were not well-trained and not motivated to fight. Joachim said it was more like shooting sitting ducks. He had shot down one hundred and fifty Russians and was still fighting for his country.

Eugen, German aircraft mechanic

By now, Eugen had been exposed to influence of the Nazi movement for almost a decade. It was difficult to think back on his time with Udet and his work in the hot desert. He had never been involved in Nazi politics but had close contact with many party members. He had quietly kept their airplanes flying and had drunk liters of cognac with them. He was a great storyteller and could draw from a long line of experience. He knew more about them and their escapades than they wanted to admit.

He still worked on aircraft daily and probably knew more about German aircraft than anyone. He still made friends with everyone around him. The informers did not dare speak out against him because of his circle of friends in high places.

Eugen was worried about the way the war was going. He personally talked with the pilots before they went on their last missions, salvaged parts from their crashed airplanes and helped bury them. Every day he was on the airfield repairing a damaged airplane or supervising other Schwarzemänner.

He had enjoyed his exciting life but now his heart was heavy and a shot of cognac did not help. Someone ordering a *Kirsch* (cherry brandy) was like a stab in the heart. He remembered the good times he had with Udet and the good *Kirsch* they had drunk together.

Everyone in Europe knew that the Allies were planning on invading Europe. The big question was, when? Everyone expected the German military to have contingency plans in place. Obviously the defending forces on the beaches knew what was happening.

But behind them was chaos. Much of it was caused by sabotage and bombing. Hitler had instilled so much fear in his commanding officers, that no one would give the order to move units to where they were needed.

Because no one wanted to be the one to disobey his orders, Hitler slept through the critical first hours of the invasion. Rommel, the man responsible for building the defenses on the beach had said they needed enough ammunition to be able to fire their guns for seventy-two hours. They had enough for six hours at Omaha beach after which American soldiers moved inland, despite taking thousands of causalities.

Werner

Werner had received the news of the invasion early in the morning. He had only eighty fighters that he could deploy immediately and most of them were overwhelmed before they could arrive over the invasion fleet. Most of his fighters were deployed all over Germany in order to defend against bomber raids.

Reports from the front told him that all the airfields that he had planned on using in that area were destroyed. Most of his communications were gone. Before he could make plans to send fighters to help, he received reports of bombers headed for Germany. He gave commands to different *Gruppe* to intercept. Every *Gruppe* reported back that they could not use all their planes because they were short of fuel.

The American Eighth Air Force could fly with little opposition over Europe. Werner was helpless to interfere. The orders to start the defense against the invasion did not come until the day after it had started!

Werner felt literally sick; the Luftwaffe had been such as beautiful organization. Its command structure had operated like a well-oiled machine. Werner could give an order and in a few minutes fighters would be airborne, knowing where to intercept the enemy forces. Now it appeared that there was nothing left of that organization. The orders from Hitler and Goering had always been misleading and confusing, but the chain of command had always managed to absorb the orders and give them direction. Now that organization was a smoking rubble like many German cities.

A gloom settled over all the German military forces, but they started to rebuild airplanes and trained a large number of pilots in a short time. The Americans assumed that the Luftwaffe was finished as a fighting force and thought the battle was over. The Americans thought that since they had seen so little of the Luftwaffe on D- Day, it no longer existed. They presumed that they had destroyed much of the German manufacturing facilities.

But the production of airplanes continued in hidden and underground factories. There were plenty of workers to build airplanes. Many were slave laborers from other countries and German political prisoners.

Some tried to sabotage their work but enough was accomplished to produce more fighters than Werner had pilots. Werner's pilots were kept busy. The Americans already had built airfields in France and were close enough to fly tactical missions even closer to the front lines. The month of June 1944 was a terrible month for the Luftwaffe. They lost one thousand airplanes even as their factories produced more airplanes than ever.

With the fall of Paris to the Allies, the Luftwaffe's morale fell dramatically. The sky was full of enemy airplanes, and there were bombing raids almost every day. They were receiving mail from home telling of the suffering of the civilians.

Bombarded by reproach from above and angered by the disrepute into which it had fallen, the feeling of inferiority, heavy losses and hopelessness of the fighting were clear to everyone. This state of mind had been brought to every German, but it gave the Luftwaffe a sense of solidarity never experienced before. Many more young men volunteered to enter pilot training and the Hitler youth were preparing to fight to the end.

Still, the Luftwaffe had to face reality. With the sky full of enemy aircraft and many of them were looking for targets on the ground, it was necessary for Werner to give the order to find places in the forest to hide his fighters when they weren't airborne.

Allied Commanders had given the order to shoot at any target that moved. It wasn't that easy, since the Germans had anti-aircraft guns scattered all over the countryside. Many of the gunners had years of experience shooting at fast-moving targets. Some of the larger guns had a range as high as twenty- thousand feet.

After the arrival of the P-51s many of the P-47s were assigned to fly ground support. For an American fighter pilot it was a disappointing, but also extremely dangerous assignment.

Emil

In spite of the allied control of the air, in the month of August 1944 the Luftwaffe received one thousand new pilots, fresh out of training. Emil could only stare in disbelief. Some were experienced bomber pilots who had been retrained to fly fighters. They knew how to land and take off, they sometimes had years of flying experience, but had trouble with the quick and tight turns required for a fighter.

The younger pilots lacked even some of the basic skills of flying. They were very enthusiastic and had little fear. Emil said to one of his close friends that they would have made excellent suicide pilots! Little did he know that when someone suggested that the Luftwaffe use suicide tactics to Hitler, he rejected the idea.

Emil went to work showing them the skills they would need to survive combat. He trained most of the pilots himself and there was usually a beginner flying as his wing man. He used straggling bombers as targets for the beginners to practice on.

One day, returning from a mission, Emil spotted a lone B-24 bomber with smoke trailing out of one engine. He had two new pilots with him and he ordered them to attack. When he saw the fighters approaching, the bomber pilot immediately jettisoned his bombs. They landed in an empty field and exploded as they walked across the ground.

The bomber went down in flames and the young pilots cried, "*Horrido*."

After Emil landed and filed his report, the operations officer comment that an Ami bomber had laid a string of bombs across two buried pipes in the Nuremberg area. Both pipes carried large amounts of aviation fuel.

The officer commented, "How could the Amis have known the location of the buried pipelines?"

Emil mumbled something under his breath and make a quick exit.

The operations officer shouted to Emil as he was leaving, "Don't plan on flying for a while; we won't have any fuel for at least ten days."

Emil was thankful that the officer had not noticed the location of the bomber his *Staffel* had shot down. He knew that if the *Amis* were allowed to fly without any opposition for ten days it was going to be very difficult to gain back control of the skies over Germany. It was worse than he could have imagined.

The Allies had plenty of aviation fuel. A pipeline from England through the English channel to France allowed the Americans to station fighters on the continent further extending the distance they could fly into Germany. Many of the bombing raids had one thousand bombers in them.

The months following the invasion, the Luftwaffe lost a thousand airplanes a month. The Germans just increased production and built a thousand airplanes a month. The time lost because of the bombed pipeline did not help because the Allies were that much stronger when the Luftwaffe could fly again. The young Luftwaffe pilots had more fighting spirit than ability. If they were not lost in combat they crashed during landing.

Kurt

Kurt had long lost any capacity for caring about what was going on around him. Personally, his flying ability was at its peak. Attacking *Ami* bombers through a hail of bullets did not register as fear or any other emotion, for that matter.

He did not bother to count the number of bullet holes in his fighter. He only asked the crew chief if his airplane could still fly. If not, he'd ask for one that could.

When he saw a group of new pilots nervously waiting for him to interview them, he wanted to scream at them to go away! Most of them were *Kinder* (children), just out of school. Now they were standing in front of him waiting for an assignment to fly a fighter aircraft in combat against an enemy that outnumbered them ten to one.

The enemy now had better airplanes and their beginners had far better training. Kurt felt like he was an ancient, old man compared to these *Kinder*. He had forgotten that he had also been that young when he started flying fighters. But when he began his combat career, he had over a year of training more than these beginners did.

When he had started flying combat, the Luftwaffe had been the strongest air force in the world. He was flying with some of the best fighter pilots in the world to teach and protect him. He had made enough mistakes flying to have died a hundred times.

In Russia the enemy airplanes had fled when they saw the Luftwaffe fighters. He had missed shooting down several Russian airplanes before he had finally succeeded and shot one down. After shooting down ten airplanes he had been shot down and badly injured.

Now he was sending young men into battle totally unprepared for combat. The shortage of time and instructors meant these men had no instrument training. The only way they had been told to land when clouds covered the ground was to spin their fighter through the clouds and hope they would see the ground in time to recover.

Most of the new pilots had been given very little gunnery instruction, so all Kurt could say was, "Please keep the safety on the guns at all times." He also told them to follow their leader but not too closely.

Taking a group of beginners into combat for the first time was a frightening experience. Kurt did not dare to try to bring everyone in formation. The more experienced pilots were all placed in their proper positions while he inexperienced were scattered all over the sky.

When Kurt saw the hundreds of Ami bombers, he immediately made his plans for attack using only the veteran pilots. Above, to the sides, and below the bomber formation were swarms of Ami fighters. Kurt was well aware that the Ami fighter pilots would go for the German fighters that were not in formation.

The experts heading straight for the bombers were dangerous men. Kurt still had a large number thirteen painted on the nose of his fighter, a challenge to any enemy who wanted to fight him. Kurt shot down another four-motor bomber and saw several others dropping from formation.

He did not turn back for another pass at the bomber formation and instead turned to help his inexperienced youngsters. Several had already been shot down. He could see the bright flames streaking from their fighters. Kurt was able to shoot down an Ami fighter that was stalking one of his. Since the formation was moving quickly away the Ami fighters broke off from combat and that allowed the young German pilots to escape.

Kurt was the first to land after the fight. He sat for a moment in his fighter before getting out. He could hear the engine ticking as the hot metal cooled. He wondered how many times he had heard that sound before and how many times he would hear it before he was killed.

His thoughts were broken by a loud thud and then the screeching of tearing metal. One of his *Kinder* had just crash-landed his airplane. Wearily Kurt climbed out of his fighter not wanting to see what had happened to the pilot. Then he saw the crash crew helping the pilot extract himself from the torn metal.

Kurt sighed with relief and thought, "Well, hopefully he learned something from that experience."

Before he reached the operations building he heard a loud smack, as one of the *Kinder* had forgotten to extend his landing gear and bellied his fighter onto the runway. He thought, *that was not the first time someone forgot to lower their landing gear after a combat mission.*

Werner

Werner had lost all his influence with Hitler. Goering was in a drugged stupor most of the time so he only nodded his head dejectedly while listening to Hitler order him to remove Werner from command in the Luftwaffe. Still, Werner was the most capable of commander in the Luftwaffe and even Hitler could see that could not afford to leave him on the sidelines.

Werner had never been a yes man and had continually opposed Hitler over how the new jet airplane was to be used. Now Werner was assigned to fly the *Me-262* with a group of experts. When the commander of the group was killed in a crash of his jet, Werner was put in charge. He started reassigning the best pilots he could find to fly in his *Staffel* of experts.

Kurt

Kurt was astonished when he received orders to report to Werner's unit and fly the *Me- 262*. He had heard the reports about the jet fighter and how it was one hundred and fifty miles an hour faster than the Ami P-51. He knew that the jet had its share of problems but he couldn't wait to fly it.

Emil

E mil had more combat experience than either Werner or Kurt, but since he
was still a *Feldwebel*, Werner did not want to bring him into his elite group.
Besides, he had as many kills as Kurt and he might outscore the others in the
group. Emil had a good reputation in training new pilots and his losses were below any of the other *Staffels*.'

Kriegies

Jim and his fellow prisoners could see that the war was going badly for the Germans. The food rations were smaller. Even the food for the guards and officers was restricted. The prisoners quietly cheered when they saw the large formations of American warplanes.

One day they were watching a formation of P-51s flying overhead. They could see a group of German fighters approaching the Americans. All of the sudden the prison compound was struck by several silver cylinders. The prisoners all scattered for cover, cursing the P-51 pilots for trying to kill them. The cylinders failed to explode.

Then one of the prisoners started to laugh. "Those are drop tanks that the P-51s carry to extend their range! When they saw the German fighters they all dropped their tanks at the same time. Some just happened to hit our compound."

Another prisoner mumbled, "I just hoped I won't be killed by our own people."

Still, most of the prisoners were ecstatic. They knew that American forces had landed on European shores. They had very little good information, but they knew the guards were becoming very nervous and more were becoming even friendly.

Now escape plans were discussed again. Their problem had always been, that once they escaped the compound, they had to travel a long distance in enemy-held territory. Now they would not need to travel as far to meet friendly forces.

Also, the German Army had lost large numbers of men in all the fighting. They were taking soldiers that had been guarding prisoners and placing them in the front lines. Many of the prisoners wanted to break out and head for the American lines. Some thought that it would be better to just wait until they were liberated by the advancing ground forces.

Jim was one of those who couldn't wait. He wanted to travel alone. He thought it would be easier for just one person to hide. He also knew that the Germans would have fewer men to search for him.

Now the prisoners started digging furiously on their tunnels. They waited for a night without a moon and were fortunate to get a cloudy night before long. It was also close to winter and the Austrian ground was frozen.

Jim walked a long way during the first night and made good progress. He stayed away from haystacks and farms. The frozen ground allowed him to leave no tracks. He found a little protection in a forest and hid during the day.

He was able to see far enough during daylight hours to plot his travel for the night. Of course he could not stay away from towns and houses very long because he would eventually need to find food and shelter. He made good progress the next night but was not able to find a forest to hide in before the next morning.

A farmer feeding his cows saw him crawling into a ditch. The news had been given to everyone in the area that prisoners had escaped and were on the run. The farmer notified the police and Jim was again captured and sent back to the prison compound. He was certain now that it would not be long before the war was over. All he needed to do was survive long enough to see that day. He did not know how difficult that would be.

Kurt

Kurt was tired of fighting and war, but when he saw the *Me-262* with its sleek lines and two jet engines hanging on its wings he immediately became excited. Werner explained to him how much faster it was than the Ami fighters. Kurt said that he thought the rocket launchers on the wing ruined the sleek lines of the jet. Werner was quick to explain that with the rockets he had the capability to fire long before the fifty caliber machine guns on the *Ami* bombers could fire.

Werner said that in one attack he had fired all twenty-four rockets at once and watched two bombers go down in flames. He also added that most of the pilots had trouble judging the speed difference between their jets and the slower enemy airplanes. The Luftwaffe had already lost several jets when they attacked enemy fighters from behind and had flown past them before firing their guns, giving the *Amis* the opportunity to shoot them down from behind.

Now Kurt could not wait to fly the *Me-262*. There were no two-seated jets, so everyone who wanted to fly had to do so without an instructor. When Kurt applied the power to the jet engines, he could not believe how loudly they screamed. The minute he was airborne the noise abated and he sailed through the air at a speed he could not have never imagined.

There was little vibration and the jet showed no bad characteristics. The landing was much easier that any of the other fighters he had flown, the tricycle landing gear making it simple. At the beginning of the war when German engineers had suggested putting a nose wheel on their designs Goering and Hitler had nixed the idea as a dumb Ami idea. Now all the new German designs had a wheel on the nose.

After flying the new jet, Kurt was anxious to get into combat and see what he could do with it. He spent some time talking to the Schwarzemänner to better know the machine. He did not know what troubles that would cause him later.

All the leaders in the Luftwaffe knew that the war was in its final days but did not want to admit it to anyone for fear of being accused of treason. The

Gestapo was executing deserters or anyone they thought suspicious. Hitler was long past functioning but was still able to frighten the secret service into a frenzy by killing their own people.

Men in the Gestapo trusted no one around them. The Russians in the East were pushing the German army slowly back towards Germany. The American and English Armies were pushing the German forces back toward the Rhine River. The skies over Germany were full of bombers pounding into rubble any town still standing. Still, Hitler would not give up and the fighting continued without let up.

Werner

Werner and his group of experts were still flying and shooting down Ami aircraft when they could. They hid their jets in forests close to Autobahns that still had intact sections. When there was a formation of bombers arriving, they would quickly push their jets out onto the Autobahn and take off hoping that the low-flying Ami fighters would not see them.

Once airborne they were confident that they could outrun any enemy fighter and always had a chance to break up a bomber formation. Still, it was not a job for the faint-hearted. When they flew back to their starting place there was a good chance that there might be an Ami fighter waiting to jump them as they came into land. As the vice slowly tightened it grew increasingly difficult for them to operate.

Werner was happy that he was no longer the commanding general of the fighter command. The Gestapo were still watching every move, but Werner had carefully selected every man working with him and they were careful not to say anything that would implicate their comrades in any wrongdoing. They were able to expose any Gestapo agents in their midst.

Kurt was sick of the whole war but would continue to fight as long as he was ordered to. It never occurred to him to do anything else. Emil was still flying and guiding his *Staffel* into a hopeless battle but refused to take any unnecessary chances. His head was continually turning and watching for danger in the air and on the ground. His Schwarzemänner and everyone in his *Staffel* kept him informed on the presence of the Gestapo.

Kriegies

Jim and all the prisoners had been watching the aerial combat overhead and could see that the Luftwaffe was losing badly. The guards and prison commander were suddenly very solemn and tired-looking. The prisoners had a hidden radio and they knew that the Russians were advancing in their direction. Some of the prisoners were already learning a few phrases in the Russian language just in case they woke up some morning and see Russian tanks outside their compound.

But no one was prepared for what happened next. Trucks suddenly drove into the compound and excited soldiers started loading up anything that was not bolted down. The prisoners noticed that the beds and equipment in the guards' quarters were not being loaded. Soldiers carried documents from the commandant's office to an empty field and set them on fire.

Soon the *Kriegies* were ordered into formation. The commandant told them to pack up all the clothing that they could carry and leave everything else. As they headed back to their barracks wondering what could possibly be happening, one of the guards told them that the Russian Army was closing in fast on their prison camp.

One of the *Kriegies* remarked. "Why don't we just wait here and let the Russians liberate us?"

The scowling guard replied, "You don't want to have anything to do with the Russkies. Now *mach schnell* and get what you can carry. "

At first most of the prisoners were happy to be leaving the prison camp. Then they saw the guards were leading German Shepherds and Doberman Pincers into the compound. They would soon learn to hate those dogs. The guards who had been indifferent to them before suddenly became very nervous and brutal.

It was still March in Austria and very cold. At the beginning of the march everyone was excited and glad to be free from the camp. The cold was invigorating and they marched with energy at first, but after a longer time they started to wonder where they were going and where they might spend the night.

The guards were edgy and nervous. Someone tried to ask what was going on. The guards would only answer, "*Vorwärts marsch.*"

As it grew darker and colder, reality set in and they realized that they would be sleeping outside. The only food they had was what they were carrying. The guards were afraid of the *Kriegies* because there was no fence to keep them in.

Any false move by the *Kriegies*, and the dogs were immediately called. A snarling dog would bring anyone back in line. The war was not over, and for the prisoners it would be just another horrible experience that they had to endure. The guards were as frightened as the *Kriegies* and any sudden move by the prisoners was quickly met with force.

Most of the prisoners had hoped that this episode would be over in a few days. The next morning they woke up and realized that this nightmare was still happening. Before they started marching, a truck pulled up and soldiers started passing out raw potatoes. The reality of their situation hit them with full force when they saw the guards and the Commandant gnawing on cold potatoes.

Nobody seemed to know where they were going. The Germans who had always been so organized now seemed disoriented and depressed. There was very little food and no shelter. The guards were becoming weaker right along with the prisoners.

Jim started to make plans to escape the column of prisoners. It could not be any worse if he was on his own and he would be away from the hated dogs. He knew that they had been traveling west and was certain that the American forces would be further in that direction.

Werner and Kurt

Werner and Kurt were still flying whenever they could. They both knew that the war was lost. They were being watched daily for any signs of weakness by their own countrymen. It was common knowledge that the Gestapo were executing German combat soldiers who they thought were not fighting with enough enthusiasm.

In the west it was necessary to form special groups of soldiers that were loyal to Hitler to watch other soldiers trying to surrender to the Allies. They had orders to shoot anybody who looked like they might surrender. In the east not many Germans wanted to surrender to the Russians, but they did want to go home. It was not easy for a deserter to hide. Any man who was not in uniform was suspect.

The Hitler youth were everywhere watching diligently for anyone who was not in an army unit. If a deserter went home, his neighborhood informers would be more than happy to turn him over to the Gestapo.

Werner, Kurt and Emil had long decided that they would rather die by the hand of their country's enemy, than be humiliated by being killed by their own countrymen.

Eugen

E ugen was suddenly removed from his work as a *Schwarzemann*, handed a rifle and placed in the front lines. He was now facing the Amis that he had been fighting for so long. Sitting in a foxhole, he could see *Ami* troops moving in the distance.

He had long experience with the Gestapo and informers. The group of men he was with were all men from Luftwaffe units like his. He studied each man carefully and was sure they would accept his leadership. He asked some of them if they knew which units were next to them. Most of them had no idea of who was beside them.

On the pretext of looking for cigarettes, he visited every unit in the vicinity. None were Hitler Youth or had any combat experience. One man in one of the distant units said that he had seen a German artillery unit fire on some surrendering German soldiers.

Eugen jokingly replied, "That would sure stop me from surrendering."

Back at his unit Eugen began his plan to surrender. He didn't want to surrender to the Americans as they attacked. All German units would be watching, and the Americans would get nervous and start shooting.

He decided that it would be best to find a time when everything was quiet. Many times, the infantry would plan their attacks for early in the morning. Sometimes they would attack in late afternoon. Everyone was nervous at night.

He decided that early afternoon would be a good time, just after lunch and as close to the American lines as possible. He listened carefully to the men he was with. They all wanted to surrender as soon as possible.

He started looking for anything with which to make a white flag. He was going to wait till the last possible moment before he informed his men that he was going to surrender. He did not want to give them much time to think about it.

The next morning was overcast and there was no firing from either side. After eating lunch Eugen decided to act. He stood up, pulled the white flag out of his pocket and gave the order, "*Auf gehts, wir geben auf!*" (let's go, we are surrendering) He immediately stood up and moved towards the American lines, waving the white flag vigorously. His heart pounded wildly, as he expected to be shot in the back by his countrymen, or by fire from the enemy in front. He saw his German comrades moving with him and realized that his whole unit was following him. American soldiers waited for him with rifles pointed at his chest.

A rough-looking soldier calmly said, "Get your hands over your head and keep coming this way slowly."

When Eugen looked back he could see most of the units that had been stationed around him streaming towards the American lines waving white flags. Young teenage American soldiers stared at the numbers of German soldiers coming their way. They anxiously looked at their sergeant with mouths wide open.

One of them asked, "Those Germans outnumber us; what are we going to do with them?"

The sergeant growled, "Just line them up and march them to the rear."

Eugen realized how frightened the young soldier was and said in his broken English, "Don't worry son, I'll keep these guys in line; just stay calm."

The next day, Eugen was in a compound with thousands of other German soldiers. After speaking with other prisoners he realized how lucky he had been. He was told that a group of captured Germans had been shelled by their own artillery and over four hundred had been killed. It was a relief for all the prisoners when they were sent further away from the fighting

Now for the first time in years, Eugen had time to reminisce. He had been an aircraft mechanic for over ten years. He had seen the rise of the Nazi Reich. As a young man he had worked for the famous Ernst Udet, the famous pilot in the first World War who had then traveled all over the world as a barnstormer. He'd flown in California and partied with Hollywood actors.

Eugen had personally talked and made friends with many of the high-ranking officers in the Third Reich. He had conversations with Hanna Reitsch, the test pilot on the V-1 rockets and one of the last people to see Hitler alive.

He had worked on almost every type of airplane the Luftwaffe had flown. Now he was sitting in the dirt in the middle of a prison compound wondering what the future might bring. One thing he decided not to do was to brag about

the people he had known and met during the war. He was certain that he coul
get along with the Americans if he cooperated at all times.

Jim

Jim was watching every moment for the chance to escape. Everyone was listless and tired, but. Jim kept working his way towards the end of the column.

He waited until they were in a forest on a foggy and cold day. Jim saw one of the guards take his dog to investigate something toward the front of the column. Other prisoners knew that he was planning to escape and had promised to cause a disturbance to distract the guards.

The minute the guard was looking ahead, Jim simply stepped out of the column and ducked behind a tree. He was careful to not make any more movements until the column was a long way down the road. He couldn't believe his luck. It was still early morning and he had lots of daylight left to get his bearings and plan the direction of his travel towards the front lines.

He was able to navigate through the forest easily enough. He was in a sparsely populated area, so even when he was in the open, he managed to stay out of the sight of any people who might be working there. He also did not need to travel on the roads and navigated cross country.

He did not find any food but there was plenty of water. Late in the afternoon, he spotted a small cabin at the edge of a meadow. He watched it carefully for a while and did not see anyone around it. Studying the ground around, it he did not detect any signs that someone had been there recently.

He carefully approached the cabin. The door had been nailed shut but he was able to easily break in. He decided that the cabin was used in the summer by people herding cattle in the area. There was a small stove in the middle. He was really tempted to make a warm fire, but worried the smoke might be noticed by someone who would report him.

He realized that the people who worked here in the summer also made cheese from the milk. He started opening the cabinets on the wall and found several rounds of cheese. He did not need an instruction manual to tell him what to do next.

After eating so much after a month of starvation, Jim wanted to fall asleep. His wary mind managed to keep him awake until it was dark outside. He awoke shivering from the cold. In the distance he heard a loud rumbling. Walking outside he could see flashes of light in the west. Artillery fire! The American lines must be over there in the distance.

He was almost free. The artillery fire died down but his mind was now racing with his new travel plans. His first impulse was to head straight for the American lines. Then he realized that he would first need to get through the German lines.

Now he needed to be especially careful because the closer he got to the fighting, the more German soldiers there would be. The next morning he filled his pockets with as much cheese as he could carry and headed west.

It was difficult to remain as wary as was necessary. After a short time he spotted a small farm. After observing it for a while he realized that it was deserted. There were no animals in the barn and no vehicles to be seen. There were no dogs or even cats.

Jim relaxed and started snooping through the barn. On top of a work bench he spotted a toolbox. He opened it and saw that it was filled with tools. He immediately started making plans for those tools once he was free. He already imagined showing them to admiring mechanics in the States. The box was heavy but he was determined to take it with him. The spoils of war. Right! He probably should do a little more plundering before he was free. He had to stop more often because of the weight of the box.

Jim found shelter in another abandoned cabin that night. He was exhausted from carrying the heavy toolbox, so he slept like a baby. The next morning the sun was shining. Jim wanted to admire his plunder in the bright light. He opened the toolbox and saw the shiny tools just laughing at him. He picked one up and tried to read the writing on it. He suddenly realized that his wonderful tools were all metric. He started swearing but realized that he really didn't want to carry that heavy toolbox anyway.

He ceremoniously dropped the box into a nearby drain ditch full of water and started making new plans for the future. Now he could travel much lighter and faster. As he traveled west and was able to stay in wooded areas, he noticed that there was much more traffic on the roads at night than during the day. It was all Wehrmacht; there were no civilians to be seen.

He could see American fighters bombing the German lines then watched the artillery shells dropping and exploding. Watching the fighting, Jim decided that he didn't want to walk into that. He could see that that the Germans were taking heavy losses and thought that they could not stay there very long.

He found a concealed hiding place where he thought that he would be safe. After it became too dark for the American fighters to fly, he heard trucks moving in the dark. The Wehrmacht was leaving!

Jim thought about walking to the American lines in the dark but decided against it, for fear a trigger-happy soldier mistaking him for a German. In the morning he watched the first patrols probing for Germans. The Americans had heard the German trucks leaving during the night. The soldiers were almost nonchalant as they moved forward, their sergeants shouting at them to watch what they were doing.

Jim had found a tree to hide behind and before the soldiers got too close he called out, "American POW here; don't shoot me you ugly bastards."

"Come out with your hands up, buddy," was the reply. Jim was no longer a prisoner after almost two years.

Jim was led to the rear, put in a jeep and taken to Headquarters. Before any officers had a chance to interrogate him, a GI seeing his condition handed him an open can of C rations. It was the best meal of his life!

He showed his dog tags with his name and serial number to an officer who ordered the jeep driver to take him further to the rear. Jim climbed in and was soon headed further from the war. Not far behind the lines Jim saw hundreds of men sitting in a field. They were ringed with guards armed with machine guns. The driver said that they were what was left of an Army that had once conquered most of Europe. Sitting among them, Eugen watched a jeep stop while a skinny, drawn man studied them for a moment before the Jeep moved on.

Werner and Kurt

Werner and Kurt knew that it would not be long before the war would be over. They had both been dealing with the problem that they could no longer affect the outcome of the war. They both knew that to be able live with their conscience they needed to fight to the very end.

From the beginning of the war they had expected to be killed in combat. Kurt had been injured numerous times and shot down on a regular basis. Werner had thought that Hitler would probably order him executed for insubordination. Now they faced the end of the war very much alive. They could not expect their enemies to overlook the fact that they had killed many of their young men.

The German civilians who had praised their exploits at the beginning of the war, now gave them hostile looks. After years of fighting for their country, their countrymen were now their enemies and would offer them no mercy. They knew the history of Europe and knew that when a nation lost a war that the civilian population would embrace the winners with open arms. The German military would be deserted as quickly as possible and left to defend themselves against the charges that would be brought against them.

Werner could see the flashes of light on the horizon and decided that it would not be long before the Amis overran his airfield. All his jets were hidden in the forest and he had several pilots who wanted to fly one last mission.

He gathered his *Staffel* together and said that he was going to lead one last mission and anyone who wanted to could fly with him. Since the sky was owned by the *Amis* they could not take off together. Each pilot would be on his own after takeoff.

Unknown to him, the Eighth Air force bomber command had stood down several days before, after the English Royal Air Force had said that there were no worthwhile targets for bombers left in Germany. Now the bombers that had been in England were flying back to the United States where they would be redeployed to fight the Japanese. Now there was had an eerie silence over the English countryside. Where just a few days before there had been hundreds of airplanes roaring into the sky, now only a few pigeons were circling.

Most of the pilots Werner asked wanted to fly, but Kurt had no problem refusing the offer. He had always hated the killing and he had more than enough wounds to prove he was no coward.

Werner was already in the cockpit of his *Me-262* when the *Schwarzemänner* rolled it onto the runway. He was gone in an instant, climbing as fast as he could into the clouds. On top of the clouds were swarms of *Ami* fighters just looking for something to shoot at; one fighter flying his direction fired a rocket and dove back down through the clouds. He could see bombs striking all around his airfield.

Werner followed the *Ami* fighter bombers dropping bombs on a stretch of the Autobahn, found a place to land, jumped out of his airplane and ran as fast as he could for a bomb crater. He crawled under a large metal object.

The next string of bombs exploded around him and he could hear the shrapnel from them striking the metal object. He noticed that a *Schwarzemann* was also using the same thing for protection. Werner commented to him that they were lucky to have found a piece of metal to protect them.

The *Schwarzemann* said, "*Herr General,* I think we should find a better shelter; that round metal object we are hiding under is an unexploded bomb."

The next morning Werner ordered all the *Me-262s* lined up on a taxiway with explosives attached to all of them. The order was given that the moment the *Amis* came in view, all the jets were to be blown up. Werner had all his men in their best uniforms lined up in front of a hanger. After the planes were blown up an American tank rolled up in front of the Luftwaffe men. A young lieutenant opened a hatch on the tank and gasped. He was looking at a line of German officers all wearing Knight's crosses and rows of other medals.

The lieutenant radioed his commander, "I have just captured the whole German high command."

Emil

It became clear to Emil that the command structure had broken down. He was not receiving any orders from headquarters and he could not reach anyone that knew what was going on. Now the truth was, that after seven years of combat, he was going to be in command of surrendering his *Staffel*. A man who had never risen above the rank of *Feldwebel* would be required to step up and make the decision about what to do with his command.

He was certain that the Gestapo men who had been watching him were gone, probably trying to save their own skins. The roads were crowded with individual soldiers that did not belong to any unit. There were plenty of serviceable airplanes on his airfield but the sky was full of enemy fighters.

Emil told his pilots that if they wanted to, they could take a fighter and fly closer to their home. He didn't recommend it, but several pilots took the risk anyway.

There were many serviceable vehicles in his unit and he gathered everyone together, putting men who came from the same area into the same truck. He wrote out proper orders for them and told them not to drive in the daylight.

He found a staff car, put some men from Frankfurt in it and headed south. Hopefully they would be safer surrendering individually than as a unit. In the dark Emil drove as close to the destroyed city as he could, dropping off one man at a time.

As they stepped out of the car, they would say, "*Machts gut*," and without turning around, disappear into the darkness.

About the Author

Cleve Ochs lived in Germany for ten years. During that time he worked and flew with many German veterans of World War Two. Many wanted to tell him about their experiences during that time. In ten years you can hear many war stories, some of them more than once.

Cleve is a retired farmer who lives in Klamath Falls, Oregon with his wife Annelotte. They still like to fish and hike the Cascade mountains.

First Edition
Cover design by Amygdaladesign.net[1]

---

1. http://amygdaladesign.net

Made in the USA
San Bernardino, CA
30 March 2020

66552886R00149